Thundering Glory

By

Lindsey Tregnago

Lindsey Tregnago

This book is a work of fiction. Places, events, and situations in this story are purely fictional. Any resemblance to actual persons, living or dead, is coincidental.

ISBN: 1-4033-7089-3(softcover)
ISBN: 1-4033-7088-5(electronic)

This book is printed on acid free paper.

1st Books - rev. 08/29/02

Chapter 1

All About Me

Do you know what it's like to be thrown by a horse? Well, I'll tell you- it's terrifying. At least it was the first time it happened. My brother, Shawn, and I were out on a trail ride when a bird flew up from under my mount and I got the ride of my life. It felt like I was on a shaky old roller coaster that slammed me up and down, spun me every which way then came to an abrupt stop with a sickening thud. All the air got knocked out of my lungs and it was hard to breathe for awhile. I was about five years old when that happened. That's what got me into rodeos. After I realized that no real harm had been done, I learned to love the feel of a wild animal under me and getting bucked around. It was a kind of adrenaline rush – exciting, dangerous, and, for me, addictive. I knew I could get hurt, and I sometimes did, but there was something about it that kept me coming back for more. Most people thought that I was crazy, but I didn't care. I enjoyed the rodeos. I did everything: steer wrestling, calf roping, barrel racing, and my favorite, saddle bronc. I owned six horses of my own.

My name's Jennifer and I'm fourteen. I have long, curly, dark red hair and green eyes. Everyone tells me I look exactly like my mother did. That makes me feel good. I guess I act a lot like her too. My mother died soon after I was born, so I don't remember her. Only what I've been told about her. From what people have told me, she must have been special. Growing up in a house full of boys and raised on a ranch, I was quite the tomboy. I had to be. Otherwise I would have never survived growing up with my brothers. I got into fights with them sometimes as if I was just one more brother to them. I liked it though. I would rather have been like a boy than a preppy little girl.

My brothers and I lived with our Grandparents and our Father on their Central Missouri Guest Ranch, The Shining Star. My Grandma's not the type of grandma who stayed inside all day baking cookies. She worked outside, like the rest of us, training young riders how to groom their ponies, saddle the ponies, and ride or jump. Sometimes when I got done with my chores, I liked to go down to the small arena and watch. Some of those little kids were really good and really got the ponies going fast.

My Grandpa was tall and rough looking. His hands were coarse from working on the ranch and his face was always scratchy because he needed to shave. Grandpa always wore boots and old jeans and an old cowboy hat. But Grandpa was also very kind. He loved animals and took very good care of them.

Dad was always smiling and he was rather quiet. Many people considered him a horse whisperer. He was very good at breaking horses. Dad loved to rope at rodeos and bull ride. He was once the National Bull Riding Champion. After my mother died, Dad never remarried.

I loved living on the ranch. Things weren't perfect (they never are) but things were as close as they could get to being perfect. I thought I was the luckiest girl on earth. A lot of people thought I wasn't being raised right, that I was too boyish, that I should grow up in a better environment, like the city. I told them I wasn't cut out for city-life. I would never fit in. The cities were too crowded for my liking. All they were was asphalt, cars, people and buildings. They made me nervous (although I may have been too stubborn to admit that aloud). I grew up in the country and I liked it that way. I would choose open fields hills and clear, cool streams over a city any day. That was the way God had intended for the world to be and I liked it.

So life was really good for me for a long time. I got along with my brothers (most of the time) and my family took care of me. We had more than a lot of other people had and considered myself lucky. Until the horrible accident that would change us all... forever.

Chapter 2

The New Horse

One day in June, I was out in one of the barns, cleaning out the stables. And believe me, it's not the most interesting job in the world. I let Take-Time, one of the barrel racing horses, out into the paddock behind the barn so that I could clean her stall and she could get some exercise. As soon as she realized that the lead-rope was off of her halter, she took off, galloping as fast as she could. "Crazy old mare," I mumbled to myself. I went back to her stall and started to muck it out. Most people can't stand the smell of a horse barn; personally I like it. I was used to the smell so it didn't bother me. It's really not that bad.

"Having fun are we?" a voice asked from behind me. My best friend, Sarah, stood in the doorway to the barn.

"I can hardly contain myself," I said sarcastically.

"It stinks in here," she said as she waved a hand in front of her face, as if trying to wave the smell away. "Your horses stink."

"They do not," I argued.

"Do too."

Sarah had chin-length blonde hair and dark blue eyes. She always seemed to be smiling and was all around good-natured. She was short (about five-foot-two) and liked sports. It was a wonder that the two of us ever got along, we were so different.

"Make yourself useful," I said, dumping a pitchfork full of manure and straw into the wheelbarrow. "Soap that saddle for me."

"Whatever!" Sarah scoffed.

"Please?"

She sighed heavily, but got the saddle soap and an old rag. She sat down on an old haybale and held the saddle on her lap. "Wanna go see a movie?"

I stood up straight and wiped my forehead with the back of my wrist. The gloves I had on were too big, but I wore them anyway. "What movie?"

"I dunno. How about 'Lake Placid'? That one looks good," she said as she scrubbed harder on the saddle.

"It's rated 'R' and you know their new rule. You have to be eighteen. We can go see 'The Haunting' it's rated PG-13."

"Okay. Let's go to the nine o'clock one. All right?"

"I'll have to ask. Patrick can probably take us."

"Did he get his license?" Sarah asked.

"Yeah. About a week ago."

"That's scary."

I laughed. My brother Patrick was pretty reckless at times. "Tell me about it. Are you gonna invite anyone else?"

"I did. Kelly can't come and Ana's not home."

"Ana's never home anymore. And if she is, her telephone's busy," I said.

"Are you done yet?" Sarah demanded.

"Yeah, I just have to dump this." I closed the stall door behind me and pushed the wheelbarrow out to the unused lot behind the barn where we dumped everything. Sarah followed me, picking the blue nail polish off her fingernails. "Let's go ask Grandma if I can go." Sarah nodded and we started toward the arena.

Sarah talked about her boyfriend the whole way to the arena. I didn't mind hearing about him every once in a while, but she talked about him constantly. I told her to stop, but she didn't listen to me. Nobody ever listened to me.

Angie was trotting Carolina around the arena and Grandma was telling her to keep her heels down. She used to threaten me to tie bricks to my heels if I didn't keep them down, when I was little. See? She was not the typical Grandma.

I liked to watch my younger cousin, Angie, barrel race her pinto pony, Carolina. She had an older sister, Alissa, who was my age, but Alissa couldn't come to visit us that year because she was in summer school by her own choice. That's where they're from, North Carolina, so Angie named her pony Carolina.

"Hi, Jennifer!" Angie waved to me.

I waved back.

Grandma walked over to the gate where Sarah and I stood. "Hello, girls."

"Grandma, can Sarah and I go see a movie? It's rated PG-13." I asked.

"Who's going to drive you there? Angela Fae Brittingham! Get those heels down!"

I ignored my grandma's yelling at my cousin and said, "Patrick can drive us."

"I don't mind."

"Thanks, Grandma," I said.

"Thanks, Grandma," Sarah parroted me. She always did that. She even called my dad "Dad". Everyone was used to it.

"Race ya to the house," I yelled and started to run up the small drive to the house. Sarah followed me.

The house was a two-story one, with a large front porch and a two-car garage. It was a ranch-style house, of course. It had rust colored sides with off-white trim around the windows and doors. The front door was a dark blue with glass in the middle in an oval shape.

She beat me to the house. Sarah was in a lot of sports, so she was used to running. She usually got hurt during the practices, though. She hurt her ankles a lot and even had to have surgery on her knee once, so she had to wear a knee brace at all times. But she was still faster than I was.

"I win!" she exclaimed, bouncing up and down, her short blonde hair flipping from side to side.

"Let's go see what time it is," I suggested, panting, as we went inside. We headed to the kitchen, which smelled of spaghetti and garlic bread.

"Mmmm!" Sarah said. "Smells good!"

"I hope so," Olive said. Olive was the housekeeper and was always cooking something. She was short with long brown hair and light brown eyes. She was heavy set, but she was pretty. I liked Olive; she was so caring and easy to talk to.

I looked at the clock. It was 5:30. "Where did Daddy and everybody go?"

"They went to the Macon auction. They're trying to sell that old mare, Sugar. They said they want a new stallion. That's exactly what we need around here; another mean horse."

"Our horses aren't mean!" I argued.

"Nope!" Sarah cut in. "They're stinky!"

"Are not!" I turned to Olive. "When will they be back?"

"Oh, pretty soon I hope."

"You wanna go watch MTV or something?" I asked Sarah. I would have rather watched CMT, but I knew Sarah didn't care too much for country music. She nodded in agreement. "I think I remember Daddy saying something about getting a new Quarter horse."

It wasn't until about seven in the evening when everyone, who went to the auction, got home. I heard the truck drive up and Sarah and I ran outside to get a look at the new horse. Actually, I went to get a look at the horse; Sarah went to get a look at my brothers.

"Howdy, girls!" Grandpa greeted us. I gave him a hug.

"Can I see the new horse?" I asked.

"He's in the trailer," Dad said, jerking his thumb over his shoulder towards the horse trailer.

I went to the side of the old trailer that was hitched up to Shayne's, my oldest brother, old pick-up. I couldn't see very well, so I stood up on the wheel of the trailer. There was a beautiful horse tied in the trailer. It was jet black and had fiery eyes. He was big too. I guess Wayde, the farmhand, could tell what I was thinking, because he said, "He's 16.2 hands high."

"16.2?" I shrieked. That spooked the horse because his head and ears picked up and he let out a shrill whinny. "Wow." I whispered. One hand, equaling four inches, made his back the same height as I was. "I thought you were going to get a Quarter horse."

"We thought so to," Dad said as he went around to the back of the trailer. "But when we saw this Thoroughbred, well, I couldn't pass him up. You read plenty of books. You said yourself that Thoroughbreds were the most valuable horses in the world," Dad answered as Wayde opened the back of the trailer.

"Arguably the most valuable horses," I corrected him.

Wayde unloaded the stallion and it immediately reared up. It took both Dad and Wayde to get him to calm down. Dad stood next to him, talking in a soft voice. The horse relaxed and allowed Dad to walk him to the barn. I followed close behind, but not too close, while Sarah stayed and talked to my brothers. Dad put him in a stall and quickly closed the sliding door.

"What's his name?" I asked.

"He doesn't have one. Why don't you chose it?" Dad hung the lead rope over one of the hooks next to the rest of the tack. "Nice looking three-year-old, ain't he? Can't have a nice horse like that with out a name."

I stood for a minute, thinking. "How about...hmm... I can't think of anything."

"Well, how about Thunder or Lightning?" Dad suggested as we watched the horse walk around his large box stall, sniffing everything with interest.

"Dad, it's a horse, not a form of weather," I smiled.

"Well, then you pick it, little miss smarty pants," Dad joked.

"I'll think of one later. Olive has supper waiting," I told him.

"Well, let's go. Don't want to keep Olive waiting."

After supper, Patrick drove Sarah and I to the Five and Drive.

"I'll pick you up later. I'm goin' over to Brandon's house. I'll see ya." Patrick was sixteen and had just gotten his license. He was the one that was accident-prone. More than once he broke his arm while bull riding. One time in particular, he was a rag doll, meaning he got caught in the bull rope and he couldn't get away. The bull drug him around for almost five minutes before the rodeo clowns could corner it and let Patrick loose. He owned eight of his own horses and very rarely let anyone else ride them. Patrick's favorite horse, Degenerate, was one of the orneriest colts on the ranch. But Patrick liked him. In a way, Degenerate reminded me a lot of Patrick.

Sarah and I walked into the large lobby and got our tickets. Then we went into one of the theaters. It was dark and the air was cool. We sat in the third row and I made Sarah sit on the outside. "Gee, thanks," she mumbled.

"Welcome," I whispered back.

The movie started and we settled back to watch it.

Chapter 3

The Horse Gets His Name

Sarah had her feet up in the chair through the whole movie. It was surround sound, making it even scarier. It was, by far, the scariest movie I had ever seen. I even screamed when the skeleton jumped out of the ashes of the fireplace. It was a very good movie. I left the theater trembling.

Sarah's mom came to pick her up and I had to wait another fifteen minutes before Patrick came to pick me up. He had his friends, Brandon and Trevin, with him, so I had to sit on Trevin's lap. It was fine with me; I've always liked Trevin. He had a dark tan and really short, light blonde hair with blue eyes. He was a really nice person, too. As my friend Sandra would say, "He's yummy." I don't say stupid things like that, but I did agree with her. They were blaring out the song "All Star" by "Smashmouth" when we pulled out onto the highway. Brandon and Trevin sang out the lyrics at the top of their lungs.

"She was lookin' kind'a dumb,
With her finger and her thumb
In the shape of an 'L'
On her forehead.
Well, the years start comin'
And they don't stop comin'..."

I had to laugh. Brandon absolutely could not sing. He was horrible, but he thought he was wonderful. I thought different. He was nothing compared to Shayne. Brandon was sixteen and a half and was really annoying at times. He had short, dark, curly hair and dark eyes and bad acne. I don't know why Patrick liked him so much.

"Are you laughing at my singing?" Brandon demanded.

"So?" I asked.

"I'm hurt," he said.

"She has every right to laugh at you," Patrick cut in. "You sing like a sick goat."

Brandon ignored him and went right back to singing.

"Hey now, you're an all star,
Get your game on, go play,
Hey now, you're a rock star,
Get the show on, get paid..."

"Patrick, did you see the new horse?" I shouted above the music.

"What? I couldn't hear you!" he shouted back.

I leaned over and turned the music off.

"Hey!" Trevin complained. "I like that song."

"You'll get over it," I told him. "I asked if you saw the new horse?"

"Yeah. Danny showed him to me. It'd make a real good bronco at the rodeo this next weekend," Patrick answered.

"It's too pretty to be a bronco. It looks more like a show horse. I'll bet that Shawn uses him for show jumping or something. He's so tall it wouldn't be hard for him to get over the jumps."

"Glory," Trevin mumbled. "All you Blackwells think about is horses."

Patrick ignored him. "I think Dad wants to name him Thunder."

"I don't like that name," I said.

"Well, it's Dad's horse."

"He said I could name it." Then it hit me. "Hey! Trevin, you just gave me an idea. What about Thundering Glory?" I asked.

"Hey! I kind'a like that name," Patrick said as we stopped at a traffic light. He reached over and turned the radio back on, which had switched to a new song.

"New kids on the block
Had a bunch of hits
Chinese food makes me sick..."

Trevin began to drum on my back to the beat of the music. The light changed and we sped down the street.

Chapter 4

Patrick's Reckless Driving

"Patrick! Slow down!" I yelled as we sped down the backcountry roads. We had already dropped off Brandon, so now I sat between Patrick and Trevin.

"Woo! Yeah!" Trevin screamed out the window. The windows were rolled down, making my hair swirl around my face.

"Relax, Jenn!" Patrick shouted above the noise of the radio.

"Dad will kill you if he finds out!" I argued, wishing my reckless brother would slow down.

"What he don't know, won't hurt me!" Patrick said. "Sit back and enjoy the ride." He threw his head back and laughed wickedly.

"You're evil! It's 12:30! We should go home!" I whined.

"I've got the truck all night," he grinned. I knew that grin. He was going to see just how much trouble he could get into with out getting caught. It scared me worse than the movie had.

We flew around the corner and I thought we were dead. Somehow Patrick managed to barely keep the truck on the road. I screamed and Patrick laughed again.

"Chill, Jenn," Trevin said.

"Chill? Chill!" I screamed. "My brother it trying to murder me and you say chill?" I turned to Patrick. "Stop right now, or I'll kill you if we survive this ride!"

Suddenly, as if from no where, a truck came over the hill. Patrick swerved to the right to avoid getting hit. The other truck passed, honking and the driver yelled something out the window. Patrick tried to keep the truck on the road, but it was too late. We went into the ditch and almost flipped. My head snapped forward, hit something, and then snapped back so fast with such force I thought my neck surely had to be broken. The truck stopped and we all sat in a stunned silence. It was dark and the only sounds were our breathing.

"Are you all okay?" Trevin finally asked quietly.

"I think so," I mumbled.

"Yeah," Patrick groaned. "Are you?"

Trevin took a deep breath. "Yeah." He sat up a little straighter. He was breathing pretty hard and his face was twisted in pain. "My side hurts," He groaned. "I got whip-lash too."

I could see him through a strange orange glow, which I didn't pay much attention to. My head was pounding and I felt something warm and sticky on my face. It took me a minute to realize what had happened. I touched my forehead and brought my hand down to look at it. My fingertips were red. "Patrick," I whispered. "I think I'm bleeding."

He tried to turn on the dome light, but nothing happened. The only light we had was the orange glow. He leaned closer. "Oh, man."

"What?" Trevin asked, leaning back against the seat.

"She must have hit her head on something."

Trevin tried to open his door, but it was slammed up against a tree. "Patrick, I can't get out."

"Guys, do you smell something?" I asked, sitting up.

Patrick's eyes went wide with fright. I suddenly realized what the glow was. The truck was on fire! Flames and smoke curled up from under the hood.

"Get out!" I screamed.

Patrick jerked frantically on the door handle. "It's jammed shut!"

"What?" Trevin cried.

The flames were beginning to get bigger and the smoke was getting thicker. I was having trouble breathing.

"Patrick! Stop playing! Open the door!" I demanded.

"I'm not playing! It won't open!" He jerked harder on the handle.

"Patrick! Hurry! Get it open!" Trevin yelled.

I started to cough. The smoke made my eyes tear and it was getting harder to see. "Open it! Open it!"

"I can't!" Patrick turned sideways in his seat and kicked at the door with both of his feet. All it did was make a horribly loud sound, which made my head pound even harder.

I started to panic. "Oh, man. Oh, man. Oh, man."

Trevin tried his door, forgetting it was pushed up against a tree.

Patrick continued to kick at his door. Then he got an idea. He tried to break the back window, but he couldn't. Not with his bare hands and he couldn't turn around and kick the window. I reached down to the floorboard, trying to find something, anything that would help. My fingers brushed something. I picked it up. "Here!" I handed the hoof trimmers to my brother.

He took them and slammed through the glass. He completely broke out the window before he climbed out. Trevin climbed out after him. That was when I realized that my purse was on the floor. I looked for it, but couldn't find it. Trevin turned around in the truck bed and reached in to help me out.

"C'mon!" he shouted.

"I can't find my purse!" I yelled. I had to find it. My favorite picture of my mom was in there. "It has my Garth Brooks C.D. in it!"

Trevin was practically crying. "Jenny, please! Please! I'll buy you another C.D. Get out! Just get out!"

I felt the strap and yanked the purse from the floorboard. "Okay!" I turned to climb out the window. Trevin pulled me out by my upper arms. As soon as I got out of the cab, we jumped out of the truck bed and ran. Every step I took hurt more then the last, but I knew I had to be as far away from that truck as I could possibly get. We reached an open field on a hill and we could see the truck from there. I knew it was coming, but it still startled me when it happened. There was an explosion and bits of glass and metal flew everywhere. The sound reminded me of the cannon at the Missouri Tigers' football games. It made me scream and jump in the air. Trevin took a few steps forward in fascination. Patrick was behind us, looking at the sky. He wouldn't even look at the truck, which, by this time, was completely engulfed in flames.

I walked up to my brother. "Are you okay?" I whispered as the flames roared behind us.

He shook his head no. "I almost killed us. I should have slowed down like you told me to."

"Hey, we're okay," I said, trying to sound brave. "I'm not hurt, I've gotten hurt worse than this in a rodeo. Remember when I fell off my horse and hit my head on the barrel? It's no worse than that."

"You were in the hospital with a severe head injury for a week, " he mumbled.

"Okay, maybe that wasn't the best example, but what the point is, is that we're okay."

"You're sure you're all right?"

"I'm fine."

We walked over to where Trevin was standing. He let out a long, low whistle. "Shayne's gonna kill you."

"That truck was a piece of junk anyway," I said, trying not to make Patrick feel guilty. "Shayne has a good truck at home."

"I'm not worried about Shayne," Patrick said. "I'm worried about Dad. He's gonna ground me for sure."

"Should we call the fire department?" I asked.

"Yeah. There's a house over there. Let's see if we can use their phone," Patrick answered.

We slowly walked to the house. I was sore and I could tell that Trevin and Patrick were too. When we knocked on the door and asked to use the phone to call the fire department, the old man, who had answered the door, said that he already had called. They were at the scene within the next ten minutes. There was also an ambulance and two patrol cars. The police questioned Patrick and the old man about what had happened while the paramedics looked Trevin and I all over for injuries. They also looked at Patrick to make sure he was okay. Trevin had a bruised rib cage, a bump on his head and bad whiplash. Patrick's eye had been bruised and had already swollen shut. He got lucky. The steering wheel had broken the impact he would have had on the dashboard. He had also bit his tongue almost all the way through, so it was hard for him to talk. He didn't get so lucky there. I had hit my head on the windshield, got cut and had a slight concussion. I also jammed my wrist, but other than that, we were okay. Nothing permanent. Nothing serious.

I got really dizzy on the way home because of the painkillers the medical personnel had given me. I almost got sick in the back of the patrol car. I lay down in the back of the car and rested my head on Patrick's lap. He didn't seem to notice and just stared out the window the whole way. I fell asleep before they even got half way to our house.

Chapter 5

The Accident

I woke up late the next day, but my head still ached. Blake was sitting on my bed. "Hey," He whispered. Blake was seventeen. He was hardly ever serious about anything. He was crazy, reckless, daring, and, at times, it seemed, insane. He was always inventing things, namely ways for us to get into trouble. He had very short, dark hair. His bright crystal blue eyes always seemed to be dancing. You could tell when he was coming up with something to get us into trouble, because his eyes would light up and he would get a big grin on his face. Blake was the type that could get away with anything and everything and never got into trouble. I think he was everyone's favorite brother. He had an identical twin, named Bryson.

I smiled.

"You feel okay? Do you hurt anywhere?" He asked.

"My head feels horrible." It took me a while to even remember what had happened. "Is Patrick okay?"

"He's fine," Blake answered. "He got his license taken away by the police. The only time he can drive is when Dad is with him. He has to feed and water all the cattle by himself and clean out the barn by himself for the next two weeks."

"I told him to slow down," I mumbled, my head aching.

"What exactly happened?" Blake wanted to know.

I explained everything, starting with when Patrick had picked me up at the Five and Drive.

I wasn't allowed to ride for two weeks after the wreck for two reasons. One reason: they wanted to make sure my concussion was gone and the second reason; just for being in the truck with Patrick, which I thought was unfair. It made me really mad because I missed the Midway Rodeo in Boone county. Patrick and I had really wanted to go.

I spent those two weeks helping Olive in the kitchen and watching Grandma and the young riders. Angie really got on my nerves because every time I turned around, she was right there wanting to play "Candy Land". I'm not really interested in board games. The first couple of times it was okay, but after eight games of candy land, straight in a row, it got really old.

One day I asked Grandma when Angie was going home.

"She's here until school starts, you know that," Grandma answered.

"When does school start in North Carolina?" I asked.

"About the same time it starts here, I suppose. Why?"

"She's driving me crazy," I said casually.

"That's a very rude thing to say. I thought you liked her."

"I like to watch her ride. Every time I turn around, she's right there. I can't take it anymore!"

"If you really want to get away from her, why don't you go down to the arena? Your Dad is trying to break that new horse they bought."

I took off out the door and down the drive to the arena. Dad, Wayde, and Danny were in the arena, trying to stop the stallion from galloping around the rail. Thundering Glory was really fast.

Jeremy was standing on the gate, watching. Jeremy was also seventeen, but he was ten months older than Blake and Bryson. He was the jock in the family. He was the captain of the football team. All the girls at school adored him, and he was all they talked about. He was tall, tanned and muscular with dark brown hair and sparkling green eyes. He only went trail riding because he thought that rodeos could, "Put his football career in jeopardy." We liked to tease him and say that it wouldn't hurt anything if he hit his head. He was wearing his football jersey and had a football in his hand. I rolled my eyes when I saw Mandy, his airheaded, cheerleader girlfriend. I hated that stupid little rah-rah. She looked totally bored at the sight of the horse and couldn't have cared less when I walked up to the gate. At first, she pretended she didn't even see me. She finally noticed me when Jeremy nodded at me.

"Oh, hi!" she greeted me in such a fake voice, I could have thrown up.

"Hi," I mumbled.

"You're not going in there with that thing, are you?" she asked.

"It's not a thing," I said as I climbed the gate. "It's a horse." I quickly walked to where Danny was standing.

"Hey, Jenn," he said, watching the horse gallop around us as Dad walked calmly behind it.

"Having problems?" I asked, giggling.

"Shut up. This horse is psycho. He sure is fast, though. Man, look at him go," Danny said. He hadn't taken his eyes off the horse since I had gotten there. I could tell that Danny was thinking about the races at the horse shows we went to. Danny loved to race, especially while riding his favorite horse, Double J. I never liked Double J very much, he bit and kicked people. But Danny liked him. Danny was fifteen and had bright red hair and green eyes.

"He'll never be broke in time," I said, reading my brother's mind.

"I know," Danny sighed. "Maybe he will. He will by next year."

"Everybody, out of the arena!" Dad commanded.

We hurried out. Jeremy and Mandy had already left. The stallion finally stopped in one corner of the arena. Slowly, Dad walked closer to him, holding a halter behind his back. Thundering Glory raised his head and picked up his ears, but he didn't bolt. Dad walked up to him and slipped the blue halter over Thundering Glory's head. Dad spoke quietly to him then began to walk the horse around the arena to cool him down.

"Jack certainly has a way with animals," Wayde said to me.

"Uh-huh. Dad's the best," I agreed. I watched the beautiful black horse trot around, holding his head up and carrying himself perfectly. "I'm gonna see what Blake's doing."

It took me awhile to find Blake, but I finally found him in the barn, talking to Patrick. Patrick was shoveling out the stalls. Out of the corner of my eye, I saw Danny running to the house.

"... So anyway, I think the Undertaker will win the first blood match. Stone Cold's forehead has already been cut open and has been cut open every week for the past three weeks," Blake was saying.

"No way," Patrick argued. "The Rattlesnake, Stone Cold Steve Austin will win. He's the fan fave."

"Fan fave has nothing to do with it. His head's been busted open and the 'Taker is going to win."

"You wanna make a bet? I'll bet you ten bucks that Stone Cold wins the match."

"You're on," Blake said and they shook hands. "Oh hi, Baby Sis. I didn't even see you standing there."

I shrugged. They always called me Baby Sis. It was sort of a nickname. "Blake, you're gonna lose that bet. Wrestling is fake anyway."

"No it's not," Blake argued.

"The fun part of wrestling is pretending it's real," Patrick laughed. "Let's change the subject, shall we?"

"What's that sound?" Blake asked.

"It's only and ambulance," Patrick said.

"They drive by here all the time," I added.

"Yeah, but they usually don't sound that close," Blake mumbled. "Maybe it's my imagination."

But a few seconds later we heard the sounds of a vehicle in our driveway and car doors slamming.

"What in the world-?" Patrick started out the doors of the barn with Blake and I following.

Parked in front of the house was an ambulance with its red and blue lights flashing.

"Oh, no," I heard Blake murmur. He took off running down towards the arena.

"Where are you going?" I called after him.

"To get Dad!" he hollered back.

Patrick and I ran into the house. No one was inside. "What in the world is going on here?" Patrick demanded.

"You don't think this could have anything to do with Thundering Glory, do you?" I asked.

Patrick eyes went wide and, without answering, he turned and ran out of the house.

Just then, Shayne came up the stairs from the basement. "What's goin' on?" he asked.

"We don't know," I answered. "There's an ambulance parked outside and we can't figure out why."

Shayne yawned. "Let's go see why it's out there then."

We walked out the door just in time to see our Dad on a stretcher, being loaded into the back of the ambulance. Then they drove off; the red and blue lights flashing and the siren blaring made me shudder. I hoped Dad would be okay.

"Danny! What happened?" I asked as he walked up to me.

"That horse," Danny said angrily, "attacked Dad. It reared up and knocked Dad over then came down on Dad's back. Dad was unconscious when we called the ambulance. I hope he'll be okay."

"Oh, no," I walked over to Wayde who had just finished talking to Shayne. "Wayde, is Dad going to be okay?"

Wayde had a grim look on his face. "I don't know, sweetheart. I don't know."

Just then Bryson came storming out of the house. "I'm goin' to the hospital. I knew that horse was going to be trouble. I knew it! C'mon, Shayne!" Bryson was very angry. I hadn't seen him so angry in a long time. He stormed over to his new, yellow, sports car and slammed the door when he got in it.

Bryson was Blake's twin brother. I had always thought of Bryson as the "Evil Twin". Bryson had the same blue eyes as Blake and the same short, dark hair, but there was something a little different about Bryson's eyes. His eyes were cold and hateful. He had a terrible temper and he hated horses. Bryson was always a little slow in school, but he tried really hard and got good grades. Bryson didn't like to talk very much, either. When he did it was usually negative.

Shayne walked by, yelling, "If anything happens to Dad, that horse is glue!" He got into the car and they drove off in a cloud of dust. Shayne was the oldest, nineteen, with thick, wavy, sandy brown hair and blue-green eyes. There had always seemed to be a barrier between us. I think he blamed me for our mother's death, even though he never actually said it aloud. Shayne was also the best singer I knew. Sometimes, after rodeos, he would sing country songs at the dances. He also had a bad temper.

I was so upset that I ran into the barn and up into the hayloft so that no one would see me cry. I hated to let anyone see me cry. I threw myself into the hay, near the edge of the loft, and looked down to see the horses. Degenerate was pacing around his stall, waiting to be let out for the afternoon.

Danny came into the barn, leading Thundering Glory to his stall. The horse walked like it was the tamest animal in the world, then nickered as if to ask, "Did I do something wrong?" Danny slammed the stall door, hung up the lead rope, and then left the barn. Slowly, I climbed down from the loft, gripping the sides of the ladder. I gripped them so hard, my knuckles were white. I walked over to the stall. I grabbed a lunge-line whip. I was so angry; I wanted to kill that horse! I stood in front of the stall, staring at the horse. Then, for some reason, all the anger went away. I was confused and I still had tears streaming down my cheeks. I looked at the horse's big, brown eyes and I dropped the whip. I carefully opened the door and went into the stall with the massive animal. He started to turn to kick me, but I smacked him. I expected to get the beating of my life, but instead, he turned and rubbed his nose on my shoulder. I scratched him behind his ears.

"You're really not so tough, are you?" I whispered to him. I didn't want to take any chances, so I left the stall. He seemed sad to see me go, but I didn't care. There was work to be done and it needed to be done before Dad got home from the hospital. I turned Degenerate loose in the field, then finished Patrick's job of shoveling out the stalls. It took me a few hours to finish the job and when I got done, it was almost dark outside. I looked towards the house and saw Bryson's sports car in the driveway. I started towards the house, happy that they were home. I knew Dad wouldn't be with them, but maybe they had good news.

I was almost to the house when someone grabbed my arm.

I cried out in surprise. "Oh! Danny, I didn't see you there."

Light shone through the windows where Danny and I stood. Even with the small amount of light, I could see that Danny's eyes were teary and bloodshot. “Jenn,” he said quietly, "I have to tell you something before you go inside."

"What?" I asked, suddenly very concerned. Danny hardly ever cried. I knew something had to be wrong.

"It's about Dad," Danny said, "Shayne and Bryson just got home. I've never seen Shayne cry before."

That was when I realized it was really bad. "Danny! Get to the point!" I almost shouted.

"They did all they could," Danny went on, as if he were talking to himself. He took a deep breath before he said, "Jenny, Dad died at the hospital. His back was broken and he had brain damage. It was much worse then we thought. There was nothing they could do."

I felt as if a sledgehammer had hit me. Everything seemed to spin and nothing made sense. Danny was saying something about Bryson, but it didn't make any sense. My knees gave out and I stayed there, on my knees, on the ground, bawling my eyes out.

"Jenn!" Danny cried in alarm. "Are you okay?"

"I just found out my father is dead, Danny!" I screamed at him. "Do you think I'm okay?"

Danny stood there quietly as I continued to cry. "Let's go inside," he finally said.

"No," I whispered, shaking my head.

"C'mon, Jenny," Danny insisted, pulling on my arm for me to stand.

"No!" I shouted and snatched my arm away.

"Fine," Danny said and went into the house.

My crying made my eyes and lungs hurt because I cried so hard. I was hurt that Danny had left me there alone. I was angry with the doctors for not doing a better job. But I was the angriest at myself for leaving Dad alone with Thundering Glory. I convinced myself it was my fault. Never once did it cross my mind that this was the horse's fault. I heard the front door open and slam shut and I heard footsteps on the porch.

"Get up," Came Shayne's stern voice.

I shook my head.

"C'mon, Baby Sis," Patrick's kind voice was right next to my ear, "Let's go inside," it whispered.

"Why Dad?" I sobbed. "Why did it have to be Dad?"

"I don't know," Patrick said quietly. I didn't look at him, but I could tell that he was crying, too.

"But, h-he was our d-dad," I cried. Patrick threw his arms around me and hugged me tightly.

"I know," he whispered. "I know."

I cried, leaning my head on his shoulder. I could feel him taking deep breaths and continuing to cry. He shuddered violently. Then there was another body next to us and I knew it was Blake. He hugged me too. We broke apart and Shayne dropped to his knees between Patrick and Blake.

"C'mon, Jennifer. We all need to go inside and get some sleep. It's been a long day," he said, his voice low. "Let's go inside."

Again, I shook my head.

"Jennifer, please?" Blake asked. "Please come inside. Will you?"

I sat for a moment, then finally nodded. Shayne smiled and got to his feet. I didn't stand up. Shayne reached down, picked me up, and carried me inside, up the stairs to my room. He sat me down on my bed. "Goodnight, Baby Sis."

"Night," I mumbled. Shayne left my room and turned off the light.

I took a deep breath and shuddered. Then I slipped my boots off, took the scrunchie out of my hair and lay down in my bed. I didn't change my clothes, because I was too tired. I cried myself to sleep that night wishing my dad would be there in the morning when I woke up. But I knew he wouldn't be.

Chapter 6

Alissa

I really don't remember the funeral very much; it all seemed like a bad dream. I remember everybody coming by and giving me hugs; people I didn't even know. Everybody kept saying how sorry they were for me, but I couldn't say anything. I just tried to smile and nod at what they said. That used to be a joke between Blake and me. "At a family reunion, when you don't have a clue who anybody is, just smile and nod. Smile and nod;" he would say. That's what I did. But every time I tried to smile, I would start to cry again. Shayne stood to my right, standing as still as a statue. He didn't cry, he didn't do anything, except stand there, shaking hands with people as they walked by. Sarah came by with her parents, but she didn't say anything. She hugged me and gave Shayne a quick hug. I could tell she was uncomfortable and I didn't blame her. I always felt uncomfortable at these things too. But now it was different. This time it was my brothers and I standing at the front of the room while everyone hugged us and talked to each other about our family. I over heard one woman talking to another about us.

"Well, you can't say it wasn't bound to happen. With all those crazy animals they have around there, it's a wonder it didn't happen sooner," the first woman said.

"Well at least one of those Blackwell children has something broken or bruised," the second woman said, looking at Patrick's eye, which had almost healed.

"If Elizabeth were still around, I'll bet they wouldn't be behaving that way."

"What did she die of?"

"She died right after she had the little girl."

"That was such a shame. And now look how that girl has turned out. She acts as if she's a boy. Always out riding those horses they keep around there, getting hurt in rodeos."

"I don't know about that family sometimes."

"You know it was a horse that killed Jack..."

I quit listening after that. I couldn't stand hearing people talk about my family that way. Talking about me, I didn't care. Most of what they said about me was true and I wouldn't deny it. But talking about my family was different. Breaking horses and raising cattle was what my family did for a living. Without the ranch, the town would have lost a lot of business. They just didn't realize how much business the ranch brought to them. Especially during the summer time.

I guess Shayne noticed how upset I was getting because he said, "Why don't you go outside for a while?"

I nodded and made my way through the people to the door. I sat on the concrete steps in front of the church. I stared at the ground trying to forget what the two ladies had said. But it kept burning in my mind. Maybe I was too much of a tomboy, I decided. Maybe I should act more like a girl. I wondered about my mother's funeral. Was it like this one? What did everyone say about her? What had they said about me? Did everyone blame me for it, the way Shayne had?

After the funeral, several relatives and close family friends came over for lunch. I've never seen so much food all at once. But I wasn't hungry. Grandpa tried to get me to eat something, but I couldn't. I found my cousin, Alissa, and Sarah and talked to them awhile.

"I'm sorry about your dad," Sarah mumbled.

"Don't be. It wasn't anyone's fault," I told her.

"I haven't been here for a long time," Alissa said.

"How come Angie came and you didn't?" I asked.

"I was busy with summer school. I wanted to come, but I couldn't. I get out of school and come up here for a couple of days, but then I have to go back," Alissa answered.

"Can't you stay longer?" I asked.

"I wish," Alissa said, "I don't have to go to summer school. I went by choice, because some of my friends wanted to go and they talked me into it. I could probably quit if I wanted to."

"Why don't you ask if you can stay the rest of the summer?" I suggested.

"Maybe I'll ask later. Not right now. Not with all the people here. It would be a 'no' for sure," she answered. "Can we go see the horses?"

"Sure," I shrugged.

We walked out of the house and down to the barn. The horses hadn't been taken care of for a couple of days and it showed. They were dirty and the barn reeked of manure.

"Man, I've got my work cut out for me tomorrow. It's my turn to clean the barn," I sighed, staring at my new black dress shoes.

"Is that all you do?" Sarah asked, "Clean the horse barn?'

"Pretty much."

"I help clean the stables back home," Alissa said.

"Where are you from again?' Sarah asked.

"North Carolina. I mainly ride English style though. I jump horses and show them," Alissa said.

"Shawn rides English, doesn't he, Jennifer?" Sarah asked.

"Yeah, but I don't like his horses. I'll ride Sable every now and then, but I don't enjoy it very much," I said. By that time, we had reached the end of the barn.

"Which horse is this?" Alissa asked. "It's pretty."

"This," I sighed, "is Thundering Glory."

"The one that killed your Dad?" Sarah asked.

I nodded. I still couldn't believe that Dad was dead. "It's funny," I said, "I don't feel like Dad is actually dead. It feels like he should still be here."

Neither Alissa nor Sarah said anything.

"Dad was trying to break him. I don't know what went wrong," I went on.

"I've helped break a horse before," Alissa said.

"So have I," I told her. "Nothing really bad has ever happened like this before. Not this bad..."

Sarah stepped forward and petted the horse through the bars of the stall. "He sure is pretty." She turned to me. "Can we go up in the hay loft?"

"Sure."

We climbed the old wooden ladder to the loft.

I sighed and flopped down in the hay. “I just can’t get over this.”

“You probably never completely will,” Alissa told me honestly.

I nodded, knowing she was right. “Why would God let something like this happen?”

“I don’t know,” Alissa answered.

“It’s not fair!” I cried, tears beginning to stream from my eyes again.

“Why don’t you ask him to help you through it?” Sarah suggested.

“Huh?” I asked, looking up, wiping my eyes.

“Ask God to help you,” Sarah said.

“Okay,” I said and bowed my head.

"What's this for?" Alissa asked, after I had finished praying and reopened my eyes. She was holding the rope that was tied to the rafter in the center of the barn.

"That's the swing Blake broke his leg on," I answered.

"That was so funny. I remember when you told me about that. We didn't let him live it down for a year," Sarah giggled.

"I remember now," Alissa said. "I'll bet if we shorten it and tie an old tire to it or something, it'd work real well."

"There's an old knife over there. You and Sarah cut it and I'll go get a tire," I instructed. I climbed out of the loft and went to the back of the barn. There were several tires leaned against the wall. I grabbed one and rolled it into the barn. It was hard to get the tire into the loft, but, eventually, Sarah and I got it up there. My Australian cattle dog, Max, watched from the floor. We let the swing go on it's own before anyone tried it. It worked perfectly. They made me try it first to make sure it was safe. Max chased us as we swung by, but he finally gave up and lay in front of Degenerate's stall.

We took turns swinging on it until Angie came out to the barn.

"I wanna try!" she cried.

"No!" Alissa argued. "It's not for little kids."

"I'm not a little kid!" Angie insisted. "I'm six years old. I'm a big girl now!"

That's where I stepped in. "It's against the law to swing from a loft unless you're over thirteen."

"Nuh-uh! You're lying!"

"You don't want Grandma and Grandpa to get in trouble, do you?" I asked.

"Are you telling the truth?"

"You bet. You'd better go inside, now," I told her.

Angie turned around and left the barn, pouting.

"I can't believe she believed you!" Alissa said after Angie left.

"Little kids believe anything you tell them," Sarah said, then jumped from the loft, swinging down towards the floor, her skirt flapping behind her. "Cody used to believe everything I told him! Then he got older and wised up!" Cody was Sarah's little brother. I remembered the time we talked him into riding a scooter down a hill towards the woods when he was four. He slammed into a tree and had to get stitches in his chin.

Danny came into the barn.

"Hi!" Sarah shouted, swinging past him.

He waved at her and climbed into the loft. He sat on a hay bale. "Guess what, Jenn."

"What?" I asked, smiling. I was having so much fun; all my troubles had seemed to disappear.

"We're probably not going to open this year, the guest part of the ranch, I mean. Dad was usually in charge of everything. They said next year," Danny said sadly, loosening his tie.

"I guess it makes sense," I mumbled, disappointedly. I had been looking forward to meeting all the people who came to the ranch. I usually would have argued, but I was too tired with everything to even think about it.

"Alissa! Time to go!" Aunt Suzie called from the doorway. Aunt Suzie was Alissa's mother and my mother's sister.

"Ask if you can stay," I whispered to her.

Alissa nodded as she climbed down the ladder.

Chapter 7

Jennifer Makes a Decision

Alissa had to beg and plead, but finally her parents gave in. By three o'clock, everyone was gone and things finally settled down. Sarah stayed after her parents left so that she could spend the night. I tried not to think about my Dad. Bryson stayed in his room the rest of the day. He even skipped dinner.

"Can we sleep in the loft?" Sarah asked.

"You and that loft," I mumbled.

"What? It's neat up there."

"Oh, I guess."

We took our sleeping bags, pillows, c.d.'s and a radio to the loft. We set everything up, got into a hay fight, then had to redo the whole thing. I over heard Wayde talking to Grandpa.

"We certainly can't keep an animal that is dangerous around here," Grandpa was saying.

"No, sir. What are you going to do with it? Sell him? You'd be able to get a lot for him at the auction," Wayde suggested.

'Oh no!' I thought to myself. 'They can't sell him!' I wasn't angry at the horse anymore. I wanted to keep him. I had forgiven him for everything he'd done. I knew he would turn out to be a good horse, all he needed was a little bit of time.

"Bryson's pretty upset. More so than the other children. Jennifer's doing okay, I guess. I think having Alissa here has taken her mind off of Jack. Bryson is the one I'm worried about. He's talking about killing the horse."

"You aren't going to let him, are you?" Wayde asked. "It seems like such a waste, destroying such a beautiful animal."

Grandpa sighed. "I don't know who will want him after everyone hears what happened. No one wants an animal that's dangerous. Maybe it would be better to put him down."

I felt tears welling up in my eyes and there was a lump in my throat that I couldn't swallow. I couldn't let that happen. Bryson wouldn't do such a thing, would he?

"It's a shame. We'll take care of it in the morning, I guess," Wayde said.

"The only other thing we can do is sell it to the first buyer at any price," Grandpa said as he left the barn.

Wayde stayed, staring at Thundering Glory. Without even looking at the loft, he said, "Jennifer, come down here."

"How'd you know I was up there?" I asked, coming down the ladder.

"I've known you since you were born. I know these things. You're exactly like your mother," Wayde said.

I reached the stall where he was standing. "Wayde, you can't let them kill Thundering Glory!" I suddenly cried.

"It's not my decision, young 'un," he said. "It's up to your grandpa now."

"Isn't there something you can do?" I pleaded.

"I tell ya, it's not up to me. I'm just hired help. If it was up to me, I wouldn't kill it, but..." his voice trailed off.

"But what?" I asked anxiously.

"Nothin'," he said. "You go have fun with Blondie and 'Lissa. I gotta get home." Wayde lived in a small house, on our property, near the highway. It had a western look to it and it was cozy. I liked Wayde's house. He lived by himself.

I sighed and climbed back into the loft as Wayde left the barn.

"What was that all about?" Sarah asked, chewing on a piece of hay.

"Grandpa wants to sell the horse that killed Dad, Wayde apparently doesn't care, Bryson wants to blow it's brains out with a shotgun and I don't want any of those things," I answered.

"Bryson wants to shoot Thundering Glory?" Alissa asked, sitting up.

"He can't do that!" Sarah protested.

"Grandpa's not going to let him, I hope. If he does, I'll never let anyone live it down. And you both know that for a fact," I said.

"You sound like you want to keep him," Alissa said.

"I do," I answered quietly.

"You're nuts!" Sarah almost screamed, sitting up suddenly.

"I am not!" I argued. I wasn't playing around this time. Neither was Sarah.

"Are too! I'm sorry, Jennifer, but this horse obsession thing of yours is getting out of hand. You never do anything anymore! You're always too busy cleaning out the stables, brushing quarter horses, taking care of Clydesdales or painting the barn to have any fun anymore. And if you're not working, you're hurt," Sarah said. She sighed. "I don't mean to hurt your feelings, but it's true." She sounded almost apologetic.

"I can't help it if I'm horse crazy. Sarah, we can't let them do anything to Thundering Glory," I said.

"What are you thinking?" Alissa asked suspiciously.

I took a deep breath. "We should break him," I said, then waited.

There was a long silence. Sarah and Alissa both had a look of shock on their faces. No one said anything. I was suddenly uncomfortable. I had just decided that maybe I shouldn't have said anything.

Finally, Alissa blurted out, "You really are crazy!"

"Shut up. We can do it," I pleaded. "Liss, you have horses and we both ride all the time. Sarah, you ride sometimes-"

"Only when you make me," She mumbled.

"A-and I know we can do it! It'll just take a little time that's all. C'mon you guys. Please?"

"Have you ever even broke a horse before?" Sarah demanded.

"Well, no. Not exactly..."

"Then what in that messed up mind of yours makes you think that we can break it? Hello? Anybody home? Jennifer, that thing already killed your dad!"

"It was a freakin' fluke! I'm telling you; he didn't mean to hurt Dad! Besides, I've seen Wayde and Dad break horses before. We can do it. Only if we work together," I begged.

Alissa looked at her blanket for a long time. Sarah just sat and slowly shook her head. I held my breath, waiting for their answer.

Alissa took a deep breath and let it out slowly. "All right," she finally said.

"What?" Sarah shrieked.

"I'll help."

"You will?" I asked. I was surprised. Normally, no one ever went along with my crazy plans like this one. Occasionally Sarah and I would do something wild, but not like this.

Alissa nodded.

I turned to Sarah. "What about you?"

"Whatever!" she rolled her eyes. "I don't even think so."

"C'mon, Sarah. It might be fun," Alissa tired to persuade Sarah.

"Getting sent to the hospital over some stupid animal is not my idea of fun," Sarah argued.

"I'd do it for you," I said, "You know I would."

"That's because you're an idiot!" Sarah screamed back at me.

"I put up with listening to you talk about your boyfriend all the time. You can do this for me."

"I think that this is just a little bit different, don't you?" Sarah asked. "To me it is." She wasn't giving an inch. Sarah could be very stubborn at times. But I could be the same way. When we disagreed on something, we usually never reached a compromise. Occasionally we would, but usually not. I always thought I was right and Sarah always thought she was right.

"Sarah, C'mon. Please? Just help us. Please? We can't do it on our own," Alissa begged.

Sarah sighed heavily and rolled her eyes. "All right, fine! I'll do it, but it's against my will!"

I was in pure shock. She had actually agreed to do something this time.

"Yes!" Alissa and I said together.

I smiled triumphantly. "I knew you'd break one of these days. I'm always right."

"Just shut up and turn on the radio before I change my mind," she said and laid back.

Alissa pulled the C.D. player from under some of the hay. She put a C.D. in it and turned it on. We weren't allowed to have it very loud because it would spook the horses. I made myself comfortable on the sleeping bag and took the scrunchie out of my hair. I kicked off my boots and stretched. I was really tired; it had been a busy and hectic day. I tried to avoid thinking about Dad, but it was hard. I concentrated on the music and that helped me to get my mind on other things.

Chapter 8

Danny's Storytelling

"What are ya'll doin'?" Danny called from the floor.

"Listening to music, why?" I asked.

"I come bearing the gift of junk food!" he yelled and bowed.

"Toss 'em up!" Sarah yelled.

Danny threw a bag of Doritos into the hayloft and then climbed up with some soda. "You all are strange for wanting to come out here at night. It gets creepy up here in the dark."

"It does not, Danny," I mumbled, opening the bag. I took out a handful of chips, then handed the bag to Alissa.

"Does to. There's some strange things that come up here at night," he said, opening a can of soda for himself.

"Like what?" Alissa asked. I couldn't believe she was listening to him.

"Oh, you know. The usual. Or maybe I should say unusual," Danny smiled.

"Like what?" Alissa asked again.

"Well, nobody knows for sure. I've seen 'em a couple of times, and so has Wayde, but nobody really knows what they are. They're really strange looking..."

I sat and crunched on chips, listening to Danny's story. That was one of Danny's strong points. Story telling. He could come up with some wild stories.

Coming from most people, no one would believe it. But Danny had a way of making you believe him. He was a good liar. No matter what he said almost everyone believed him. I had always thought he would make a good lawyer...

"They've got long hair, if that's what you want to call it, and they walk funny. All sort'a hunched over, like an ape, but that's not what they are. They're dark colored and smell funny. I swear if the wind's blowing just right, you can smell those ugly things a mile away. Really ugly things. Just being out here, knowing that they are outside gives me chills," Danny said. He shuddered a couple of times. "Heck, they could be right outside the barn door. They could even be right under us."

"Then why can't we smell them if they're right under us?" Sarah boldly asked.

"The wind ain't blowin' in here, duh," Danny said matter-of-factly. He lowered his voice, "They could even be in the loft. No one's ever seen them in the daylight. Few people have ever even seen them. But I have. And I don't care to see them again. One time, I was out in the field and I saw them. One of them looked right at me. It was a good thing I was on horseback. Double J left 'em quick enough. But if I had been on foot..." he paused and shuddered again. "I don't even want to know what they would have done to me. That's why I don't even like the idea of being out here right now."

"You are so bad at lying," I said, trying to keep the fear out of my voice.

"No, I'm not. Remember when the White's lost those two cows and found them out in the field? They were shredded and half eaten. They could hardly tell that they were cows, except for the tags in the ears..."

"How come I didn't hear that part? Besides, it was probably just coyotes or something Danny," I said.

"Coyotes don't do that, not to cattle. Oh sure, they might do that to a rabbit or something, but a cow? C'mon, Jenn. Think about it. Some people think it's, like, big foot or something, but they aren't that tall. Some people think maybe they're descendants from a couple of gorillas that escaped from the zoo about twenty or so years ago," He said as serious as could be.

"Danny! Go away!" I shouted at him. "We don't wanna hear it!"

"Suit yourself," he shrugged. He started to climb down the ladder. "I really don't wanna stay out here any longer anyway." He shook his head, laughed and left the barn.

I looked at Alissa and Sarah. They were trying not to look scared, but I could tell that they were. Danny was so good; he had almost convinced me. I couldn't shake the feeling that we were being watched. It seemed like there was more than just me, my friends and the horses in the barn.

"He's just trying to scare us," I said.

"Yeah. And I'm tired," Sarah yawned.

"Me too," I agreed.

Alissa was lying down on her sleeping bag. I flopped back onto my bag and turned off the overhead light. It was darker in the barn than I thought it would be. The only light we had was from the full moon. It shone in through the loft door, painting the white walls a pale blue. The air had gotten slightly cooler, but it was comfortable. I yawned and wiggled around, trying to get comfortable. I finally found the right position, and I tried to fall asleep. I was exhausted, but I was kept awake by Danny's story. It kept rolling around in my head, driving me crazy. I knew it wasn't true, but Danny's voice had been so serious, so convincing. It scared me. I shivered violently as a breeze blew through the open door. I could hear my friends moving around. Alissa was turning over and over, not getting any sleep at all. Sarah had the blanket pulled up so it almost covered her head.

Suddenly, Sarah sat up. "What's that noise?"

Alissa and I sat up too. "What noise?" Alissa asked sleepily.

"Shh! Listen," Sarah said in a loud whisper. There was a long silence and nothing happened.

"Go back to sleep," I yawned. But then I heard it too. It was a rustling sound, coming from the other side of the loft.

"What is that?" Alissa asked, terrified. She clutched her blanket in her hands and pulled it up to her chin. He eyes were wide, fixed on the moving hay at the other side of the loft.

"Rrrrrraaaaaaaaaahhhhhhhh!" Three figures jumped at us from under the hay.

Sarah, Alissa and I screamed as the growling creatures came at us.

"It's the creatures Danny told us about!" Sarah screamed and pulled her blanket over her head and lied down.

The creatures stopped their attack, sat down and laughed. I reached over and flipped up the light switch.

Sarah carefully peaked out from under her blanket. She sat up quickly, yelled, "Patrick! You jerk!" and punched my brother's arm. Patrick, Blake and Trevin were covered in hay and laughing their heads off.

"Get out of here!" I yelled at them at the top of my lungs.

Alissa sat, holding her knees and trembling. She looked really scared.

"It's the creatures Danny told us about!" Patrick mimicked in a high pitched voice. Sarah hit him again. Danny stood in the middle of the doorway, leaning against it and laughing until he was blue in the face. He dropped to his knees and fell over, holding his stomach and rolling with laughter.

"How long have you been up here?" Sarah demanded.

"Long enough to hear everything that's been said," Blake laughed.

"I'm gonna kill the four of you! Get out!" I screamed at them.

They ignored me, of course. Trevin pulled pieces of hay out of his blonde hair.

"So you're really gonna try to break that horse?" Blake asked as Danny climbed into the loft.

"We're not going to try," I said, "We're going to do it."

"Good luck," Blake mumbled sarcastically.

"You're stupid," Patrick said.

"No," Sarah cut in, "You're the one that's stupid. You crashed the truck and made it explode. You practically killed everyone."

"Shut up, blonde! At least I can tell the difference between green and yellow!" Patrick shot back. That was always his defense against her.

"Patrick, you doink, she's color blind when those colors are next to each other," I reminded him.

That's where Blake and Danny started in on both of them by telling dumb blonde jokes. They went on for at least ten minutes before Sarah and I got going. We started telling jokes about women being smarter than men and other jokes.

Finally, I said, "Guys, go to bed." Reluctantly, the boys let the barn. I turned off the lights and we went to sleep.

After I realized the whole thing had been a big prank, I didn't care about the "creatures" anymore. There was one thing that bothered me: Thundering Glory. And the thought of my Dad being gone. But the day had been so long, and my pillow felt so good, I couldn't even think about it and I was asleep within a matter of minutes.

Chapter 9

The Argument

The next morning, we woke up and got dressed. Because it was so hot I put on my new, pale yellow tank top, with denim shorts and a pair of sandals. When we went inside the house, the subject at breakfast was, of course, Thundering Glory. It turned out to be one of the biggest fights I've ever had with my family.

We sat down, prayed, then began to eat.

"Well, I think we should just hold onto that horse until the Macon auction next month and try to resell him," Grandpa said.

"Kill it," Bryson said bluntly, looking at his plate. He had hardly eaten anything.

"Bryson, I already told you no," Grandpa said.

"Then I'll do it."

Grandpa sighed.

"Hey, Grandpa, did ya hear what the girls are gonna do with that horse?" Patrick asked.

"No, what?" Grandpa asked.

"They wanna break it," Patrick went on.

"Patrick!" I kicked him under the table. He leaned over to rub his leg.

"I don't want anyonc going ncar that stallion, understand me?" Grandpa commanded.

No one said anything, except for Bryson's snickering.

"Jennifer, I mean it," Grandpa warned.

"I didn't say anything!" I shrieked.

"No, but you were thinking it," Shayne said.

"First of all, no one was talking to you," I shouted, pointing at Shayne, "and second, I think we should give Thundering Glory another chance."

"That horse killed our Dad and you want to give it another chance?" Bryson yelled.

"Everyone deserves another chance," I shot back.

"Not a killer horse!"

"Danny keeps Double J and it's a mean horse!"

"Don't bring me into this!" Danny yelled.

"Besides," Bryson said. "It didn't kill anyone."

"I don't think Thundering Glory meant to hurt Dad!"

"No, it was playin' with him when he landed on Dad's back!" Bryson shouted, sarcastically.

"Shut up!"

"Make me!"

"I will if you don't shut your big, fat mouth!"

"Why don't you both just shut up?" Patrick yelled. He slammed his fists one the table and stared at his plate. He was angry. Patrick never got angry. That should have been my first clue to stop. But I didn't.

"No!" I screamed and jumped up from my seat. "I don't have to!" I turned to Bryson. "I have had it with you! You have never liked horses! Why? Why do you always have to try to ruin the rodeos and shows that I go to? You don't ruin Jeremy's football games for him! You don't ruin Shayne's baseball games! Why do you ruin every sport that has horses in it for everyone else? It ain't fair! You keep away from Thundering Glory. He's my horse now. Mine! And I don't give a rat's -"

"Jennifer!" Grandma cut me off. "That is enough!"

I took a deep, angry breath and sat down. Bryson hastily got up from the table.

"That is it! I disown you! You are no longer my sister! You couldn't care less about Dad. You couldn't care less!" Bryson shouted and ran out of the room. I heard his footsteps pounding angrily on the stairs as he ran up them.

"Jennifer, I don't believe you," Grandma said. "How could you yell at your brother like that after all he's been through?"

"After all he's been through?" I demanded. "Why is he getting babied? Ya know, we're all going through this, too."

"This is so full'a crap," Blake mumbled to himself.

"You don't even care that Dad is gone," Shayne said.

That hurt. It really hurt me. I looked at Shayne and felt tears coming. Everyone sat in silence for a moment.

"Shayne!" Grandma snapped, "How could you say something like that?"

"I'll tell you how. It's the truth! She's the one that encouraged Dad about that horse. And now she wants to keep it. She's just up and running around today like nothing has happened. Having her little friends over... I'm almost sick. Our Dad is dead because of some stupid animal. I'm with Bryson. Kill it. If Bryson doesn't, I will. Either way, that horse is glue. I said it before. I'll help Bryson kill it," Shayne said.

There was a long, uncomfortable silence until I got up and left the room. I left Sarah and Alissa in the kitchen and went into the living room. I threw myself onto the couch. I stared out the large picture window. I wasn't hungry anymore. I was angry. All my muscles were tense and I felt like beating someone up. Particularly Bryson. I knew I could have if I had wanted to – he wasn't that much stronger than I was.

Everybody was against me. I had figured that at least Patrick would have jumped in and helped me, but I was alone in this fight. I was angry with Shayne and Bryson for wanting to kill Thundering Glory. I was angry with Patrick, Danny and Blake for not saying anything that would have helped me. I was angry with Shawn for not being home to take a side, but then I realized he wouldn't have done anything either. And I was mad at Jeremy for just sitting there like a bump on a log, like he had rocks for brains or something. If he even had that much of a brain at all...

I heard the front door slam shut, but I ignored it. *Maybe I should go apologize,* I thought to myself. *I shouldn't have yelled like that.* I pushed myself up from the couch and started towards the kitchen to apologize when I saw something out of the corner of my eye. Through the window I saw Bryson heading towards the barn. His eyes were fixed on the door and he held something in his hands. It took me a moment to realize what Bryson was carrying. Then it hit me.

"Wayde! Grandpa! Bryson has a gun!" I screamed and ran out the door, barefoot. I ran towards Bryson, but I tripped over a rock and fell.

I heard the door open and footsteps on the porch. Jeremy ran past me, trying to get to Bryson. Bryson paused, turned and looked then took off towards the barn at full speed. I scrambled to my feet and continued after them. Jeremy ran as hard as he could and tackled Bryson. As he did, the gun shot into the air. I screeched to a halt, hoping no one had gotten hurt. Jeremy grabbed the gun and threw it. It landed at Shayne's feet. Jeremy rolled Bryson over and punched him. Bryson fought back, but he didn't have much of a chance with Jeremy sitting on his chest. Jeremy was also a lot bigger than Bryson.

"Stop! Jeremy, quit!" I yelled. "Jeremy, get off of him!" I ran over and, grabbing Jeremy around his neck and shoulder, tried to pull him off of Bryson. Jeremy threw me off and continued to pound on Bryson.

Wayde ran over to them. "That's enough!" he yelled as he pulled my brothers apart. Shayne reached down and picked up the gun.

"Lay off of Jenn!" Jeremy shouted. "Cool it! Leave her alone!"

"Let me kill that stupid animal and then I'll cool it!" Bryson shouted back. "She doesn't even care about Dad! She does not even care!"

"What do you want me to do?" I screamed.

Wayde held Bryson by his shoulders until Bryson shook him off.

"You want me to cry?" I shouted, tears beginning to stream down my face. "Of course I care! Here!" I sobbed. "I'm crying! Are you happy? Huh? Are you happy now? I hope so!" I ran past them and into the barn. I absolutely could not stand it anymore. I went inside Thundering Glory's stall and cried into his mane. He nudged his velvety nose against my bare shoulder. I had only wanted for Jeremy to stop Bryson, not beat him up. Now Bryson would only be angrier at the horse, and at me. Thundering Glory seemed to know what was wrong, because he nickered and nipped at the bottom of my shirt.

Shayne came into the barn holding the gun. "Jennifer, I have to talk to you. Come out of the stall."

Reluctantly, I came out into the passageway of the barn. I was scared, I didn't want Shayne to hurt the horse or me. "What?" I asked, forcing my voice to stay clear.

"We cannot keep that wild animal. You and I both know it. It's too dangerous, especially with Angie running around. It wouldn't take too much to hurt her. All it would take is just one kick and…"

"So keep that brat away from my horse," I said, looking at the ground, holding onto one of the bars of the stall.

Shayne was getting impatient. "It's not your horse."

"It is now." Nothing was going to stop me. That was my horse and nobody was going to take him away from me or hurt him.

"Dang it, Jennifer! Can't you see that's a dangerous animal?"

"So is Double J and Danny gets to keep him! What about the broncos we keep up here every summer?"

"Those are different..."

"How? How Shayne? How are they different?"

"They just are! They're supposed to be mean..."

"But they're mean and can hurt people too," I cut him off again. "Shayne, please..."

Shayne gripped the rifle tighter in his hands. "Get out of my way," he said, sternly. He started towards the stall.

"No! Shayne, please! Don't-"

"Shayne!" Wayde hollered from behind us. "Go back inside. Give me that rifle."

Shayne's dark eyes flamed and burned into Wayde's, but Wayde held his ground. Shayne was gripping the rifle so tightly in his hands that his knuckles were white. He finally dropped the rifle to his side, turned and went back to the house.

"You okay?" Wayde asked.

"Why is everyone against me?" I asked.

"They ain't mad at you, sweetie, they're mad at the horse 'cause of what it did to their dad," Wayde said with his southern accent.

"Yeah? Well he was my dad too, ya know?"

"It ain't you they're mad at," Wayde insisted. "It's the horse. You can't blame them."

"But they can't blame the horse!" I shot back. "He's never made a move to hurt me." I had forgotten about Thundering Glory attempting to kick me.

"But, darlin', you don't know that he won't make a move to hurt ya," Wayde sighed.

"I guess that's just a chance I'll have to take. Nobody's gonna touch, much less hurt, my horse," I said. "Besides, we take that chance with every horse we ride. Or every time we go to a rodeo. There's always a chance that we'll get hurt!"

"You're so stubborn," Wayde smiled, shaking his head.

I smiled back at him.

He sighed, "I'll never figure you out. You're exactly like your mother."

"I'll take that as a compliment."

Wayde shook his head and left the barn. He mumbled something to himself, but I couldn't make out what he was saying.

"Are you okay?" Came Alissa's voice from behind me.

I turned around and nodded.

"Maybe we shouldn't try to break this horse," Sarah said. "Isn't there a different horse we could work with?"

"No! I won't work with another horse. I'm gonna work with this horse," I said sternly.

"But he's so big, Jenny. I'll be down right honest with ya; I'm scared of him. I really, really do not want to do this," Sarah said.

"Fine. You don't have to help me," I told her. She breathed a sigh of relief. Then I went on, "I'll do it on my own."

"But you can't do it by yourself!" Sarah whined.

"I'm going to do this with or with out your help. It's your decision. Alissa, you're still gonna help me, right?" I asked.

Alissa nodded.

"Has the whole world gone mad? Have you all gone horse-crazily insane?" Sarah demanded.

"Kit-Kat, you don't have to ride him. You can do other things," I said. I knew using her nickname would soften her up.

She stood still for a minute as if batting the idea around in her head. "Fine," she finally sighed. "But you get to pay the hospital bills when I get hurt."

"Okie-dokie," I giggled.

I could tell she didn't want to help. Not in the least. Sarah never did like horses very much. She didn't understand why I liked them at all. I didn't care. If we were going to break Thundering Glory, it was going to take time, teamwork and a lot of pain and patience. But it would be worth it, I knew it would be.

Chapter 10

Working with Thundering Glory

The next day we woke up at five in the morning. Alissa and I had to practically drag Sarah out of her bed. She was cranky.

"I don't wanna get up. Leave me alone!" she argued, pulling her blankets over her head.

"Get up!" Alissa yanked the covers off of Sarah.

Unwillingly, Sarah slowly got out of bed. Her blonde hair was sticking out all over the place and her eyes were half closed as she walked to the closet. She stayed over at my house so much that the guest bedroom was practically hers and she had some of her own clothes in it. She grabbed her glasses off of the dresser, put them on, grabbed a pair of jeans and a white T-shirt then changed. "It is too early to put in contacts," Sarah decided aloud as she brushed her hair.

"Could you possibly go any faster?" I demanded.

"Shut up," she mumbled.

When Sarah was done, we went out to the barn. She griped the whole time. "I don't want to get up this early, I don't want to be near that horse. I want to go back to bed. I don't even like horses. They're stupid. Why did I agree to this?" she asked, picking up a lead rope. "Am I stupid or something?"

"Yes," Alissa answered, turning on the water pump to water the horses.

"Okay, dude, that's, like, one of those questions you ain't supposed to answer. I wasn't even talking to you! I hate horses. I hate mornings. That horse is gonna kill me. I don't want to be here. And what the heck is that awful smell?" Sarah yelled.

"Just shut up and quit complaining. We've got to get some work done before everyone wakes up," I snapped.

Sarah rolled her eyes at me.

"I saw that." I took the lead rope from Sarah, opened Thundering Glory's stall door, and led him out. "Thank God he's halter broken at least."

I led the horse down to the arena, followed by Alissa and Sarah. Alissa carried a blue-green bareback pad. She seemed excited to help me. Sarah, on the other hand, drug her feet and seemed half-asleep and angry. We entered the arena and I tied Thundering Glory to a post. Then I took the bareback pad from Alissa and held it out to Thundering Glory so that he could smell it. After that I slowly placed it on his back. Immediately he reared and threw it off his back. I repeated the process again. And again... and again...and again...

"Let me try something," Alissa said.

"All right," I sighed. I exasperatedly handed the bareback pad to Alissa. Then I went to stand beside Sarah.

Alissa took the bareback pad and showed it to Thundering Glory. Then she loosened his lead rope so that it was much longer than I had tied it. "This way he can see what I'm doing," she explained.

"He can also bite you that way, " I warned. I always tied the rope short because I had been bitten too many times before.

"Maybe not." Then she began to lightly rub the bareback pad on Thundering Glory's neck, slowly moving to his withers, then down his front leg. She went on to his back, his back legs, then she did the other side.

"What are you doing?" Sarah asked, skeptically.

"I read this in a book. It's what they call 'sacking out the horse'. It's supposed to show him that the blanket won't hurt him." Keeping the bareback pad on him, she slowly moved it until it was sitting on his back. Then she let go. Thundering Glory didn't throw it; he just looked at it, then stood there.

My jaw dropped. "It worked! It really worked!"

Thundering Glory looked at me as if to say, "Well, duh!"

Alissa smiled proudly. Then she took the cinch. She didn't tighten the cinch, but she fastened it enough to let the horse feel it around him. Thundering Glory spooked and pulled back on the lead rope and broke it. Galloping and bucking around the arena, he tried to throw the bareback pad off.

"Oh crap!" Sarah screamed and ducked down, covering her head and neck with her arms.

"Blonde," I muttered.

Thundering Glory continued to buck. He soon quieted down and stood in a corner of the arena, his head down and a defeated look in his eyes. I slowly walked to where he stood. I was very cautious as I remembered what had happened to my father. He let me walk up to him and take the small part of the lead rope that was still attached to his halter. I talked quietly to him. "Easy, boy, easy," I whispered. I clucked to him, then walked to his side and removed the bareback pad. Then I led him to the center of the arena.

"What time is it?" Alissa asked.

"Time for you to get a watch!" Sarah said. Then she added, "It's 6:30. Can we stop now?"

"Yeah, we made a little progress, let's put him back in his stall," I said. I gave the bareback pad to Alissa and she put it in the tack shed. Then she and Sarah went back to the house. I led Thundering Glory back to the barn and took the lead rope off his halter. "Cheap piece of crap," I mumbled to myself. I brushed Thundering Glory and put him in his stall. I fed and watered him and the other horses, then went back inside to get some more sleep before everyone else woke up at 7:30.

We worked with Thundering Glory every morning for a month, getting up at 4:30 and working until 6:30 or 7:00 a.m. It made me tired, but we were making progress. We could put a bareback pad on him and cinch it up, and he wouldn't buck. He let us put a snaffle bit in his mouth, but I could tell he didn't like it.

One day we put saddle bags on top of the bareback pad.

"Gimme a couple of those bricks," I said. Alissa handed them to me and I put two in each saddlebag. The bags were old, so it didn't matter if they got dirty. "This way he'll get used to having weight on his back. Then, if he doesn't act up, we can put a saddle on him."

Thundering Glory stood straight up and moved his ears forward, but he didn't bolt. I walked him around the arena several times. The weight didn't seem to bother him.

"Can we try a saddle?" Alissa asked, excitedly.

"Well...all right. We can try it. He might go crazy, though, so be prepared," I answered.

"I'm always prepared for that horse to go crazy," Sarah yawned as Alissa walked to the tack shed to get a saddle.

"Get Shawn's!" I yelled to her.

"Which one is it?" she called back.

"One of the English saddles!"

She came out a few minutes later, carrying Shawn's English saddle and riding pad. "Why his saddle?" she asked.

"Because English saddles aren't as heavy as western ones."

"Oh," she said. "What makes western ones heavier?"

"The cantle and pommel," I said. I removed the saddle bags, laden with bricks, and the bare back pad. Then I put Shawn's saddle on his back. He turned to watch me, but he didn't react. I then walked him around with the saddle on his back. He didn't bolt, kick, or buck, even the least little bit.

"Cinch it up!" Alissa encouraged.

"No way!" I called back. I didn't want to push my luck. I was surprised that he hadn't tried to get the saddle off already. After about five minutes, I took the saddle off, brushed him down, and then let him into the paddock behind his stall to have a little freedom. He wasn't supposed to be let out, but since I was watching him, I figured it was okay. Besides, I had been breaking the rules about this horse for that past month, why should I have started worrying about it then? He ran and kicked his back feet into the air, happy to have some time to run and be free. I wished I could ride him, to just let him gallop around the ranch, but if he threw me and I got hurt, my brothers would get angry again and try to sell him. I stayed with him until I saw someone in the house getting up. I decided to put him back in his stall before we both got into trouble. He came as soon as I called him and willingly went into his stall. Then I went inside to see what was going on.

My family was discussing whether or not to have the big rodeo that we always had the first weekend in August.

"I just don't know," Grandpa sighed.

"Well, we haven't done anything else this summer," Danny grumbled.

"Why break the record?" Bryson asked.

"Ha! Remind me to laugh next time," Danny said.

"Why don't you both quit being such smart-" Shawn started.

"Shawn," Grandma warned.

"What do you think, Shayne?" Grandpa asked.

"I want to have the rodeo, but it's not up to me," he replied, looking at the newspaper.

"Well, you're the oldest, you need to make a lot more of the decisions around here now. You're kind'a in charge," Grandpa said.

"Then if I'm in charge," Shayne looked directly at me, "I say we get rid of that horse!"

"Forget about the horse for one minute," Grandpa said, waving a hand in the air. "Concentrate on the rodeo."

"Let's have it. Heck, let's go ahead and open for the rest of the season. Everyone's been callin' and wantin' to reserve certain cabins and stuff. Let's go ahead and open it. It might be a good idea," Wayde suggested.

"It's gonna take a lot of work, getting those cabins ready in time. We'd only have a small amount of time to get everything fixed up," Grandpa said.

"My friends and I can help out," I volunteered. "Sarah will help. And Alissa and I can call some other people to help. Alissa likes to clean and so does..."

"Whoa, slow down, Jenny. Let's just wait a second," Blake said and smiled. He knew how much I wanted to open the ranch. I could tell by the look on his face that he wanted to open it just as much as I did.

Shayne sighed deeply, "We sure could use the money. If you want to, Grandpa, go for it."

Grandpa smiled. "We'll start work as soon as we can get some help out here."

"Why wait?" Danny asked, excitedly, "Let's go start now!"

"Not on an empty stomach, you're not," Olive said, coming into the dining room.

"All right," Danny sighed and sat down.

"Shayne, you and Bryson go with Wayde and check on the cabins," Grandpa said between sips of coffee.

Bryson groaned and rolled his eyes," This is so stupid."

Grandpa ignored him. "Patrick, Blake and Shawn, you go clean up the guests' horse barns. Danny, you go with them. Jennifer and Alissa, I want you to saddle a couple of horses and ride along all the fencing and make sure there are not any holes in it or any broken or rotten rails. If there are, write it down and we'll fix it later. Then I want everyone to come and help load some hay and straw onto a wagon to take over to the guest barns. All right?"

We finished our breakfast, practically in silence. As soon as Alissa and I were done, we ran outside to saddle Degenerate and Take-Time. We rode quickly to the guest part of the ranch. I rode Degenerate. Alissa wanted to ride him until I told her she would probably be thrown. It didn't take her long to change her mind.

It took a long time to ride along the fence, but it was enjoyable. Luckily, there weren't many places where the fence was broken or damaged. We had fun spooking the cattle by running at them on our horses, and then we went to the old barn where we stored the hay. The barn had a metal roof and three sides made of metal, with one side open. Hay was stacked to the ceiling. To the right was a shorter roof, which covered a tractor and a large wagon. When we got there, Danny's, Patrick's, Blake's and Shawn's horses were tied outside and they were hooking the wagon to the tractor.

"Hey, Jenn!" Danny waved to me. The tractor was so loud, I barely heard him. Shawn was backing the tractor up to the trailer and Blake was motioning for Shawn to move back more or stop. When Shawn was finally close enough, they turned off the tractor.

By the time Wayde and Shayne got there, Shawn had managed to get the trailer in the right place (after several attempts). Alissa stood back and watched. Shayne was at the top of the haystack and handed down bale by bale to Blake, who handed it to Patrick, who handed it to me. Then I handed it to Danny, and he, Wayde, and Shawn placed it on the trailer. We spent the rest of the day loading the hay and driving it over to the guest part of the ranch. They let me drive it one time. After we got it to the guest barns, we would have to unload each trailer full into one of the barns. On the last load, Shayne drove and Wayde took Alissa back to the house in the truck. The rest of us climbed onto the trailer and I laid on some of the bales. Shawn, Danny, Patrick and Blake lay on the hay also. The sun had just set and the stars were beginning to shine. It was getting cooler, but it was still pretty warm. I stretched and yawned. Patrick chewed on a piece of hay and crossed his arms behind his head.

"How many stars do you think are up there?" he asked to no one in particular.

"Too many to count," Shawn yawned. Shawn was the second oldest brother. He was tall and slender with reddish-brown hair and golden brown eyes. He was more into the English side of riding than into the western.

"It sure is pretty out tonight, ain't it, Jenny?" Danny asked quietly.

"Mmm," I responded. The stars were now shining brightly above us and the crescent moon shone. A breeze came and went, carrying with it the smell of fresh grass and everything that was country. I loved nights like these, everything seemed perfect. I knew that everything would be all right, now that we were opening the ranch. Things would go back to the way they were before. Except for one thing: Dad wouldn't be with us this year. But I knew we could pull it off. I had to make him proud of me. If I could just ride Thundering Glory, Dad would be proud. I knew he would.

Chapter 11

Shopping and Swimming

We spent the next week cleaning barns, repairing cabins and fencing, and cleaning out the large arena we used for rodeos. We used the smaller one for breaking horses and Grandma used it to work with new riders. But since the ranch hadn't opened yet, Angie had been the only rider.

After word got around about the ranch opening, we received tons of letters and phone calls. It seemed like everyone wanted to reserve a cabin. Lots of people wanted to know if the rodeo was scheduled for this year. We told them yes. There were even a lot of people from other states that were coming. Our book was soon full of names and phone numbers. A lot of the time we had to call people back to let them know if there would be any place for them to stay. Some of the people that came wanted to sell their horses or cattle, some wanted to enter the rodeo, and some people just came for the fun of it.

It only took three or four days to completely fill the guest book for the next two and a half months.

I was so happy and so was Alissa. Of course, Sarah couldn't have cared less about the horses, but she was happy to be able to meet a bunch of new people.

As it came closer to time for the ranch to open, I thought that everyone had basically forgotten about Thundering Glory, who Alissa and I continued to work with. Sarah came over occasionally to help us out.

Thundering Glory didn't mind a saddle on his back, and we could cinch it up, like you're supposed to, and we could put a snaffle bit in his mouth. Neither Alissa nor I was brave enough to ride him yet. If either of us got hurt, everyone would want to know how and that would remind them of how dangerous Thundering Glory was. Or at least, how they thought he was dangerous. I thought the idea of him being a threat to anyone was stupid. It had to have been a fluke when Dad had gotten hurt.

I decided not to even mention Thundering Glory to anyone. The horse meant too much to me to have one of my brothers sell him, or worse, shoot him. I couldn't let that happen, so I tried to get everyone to forget that he existed.

One day, Grandpa told Shawn to take Blake, Patrick, Danny and I to town. Shawn took us to "Orchlen Farm & Home" to pick up some tack before the ranch opened. We each usually bought a new horse when people would bring them to the ranch to sell. Whatever a person made by selling their horse on our ranch, we got a certain percent of their profit, so we got the horses for ourselves fairly cheap. Grandpa gave a credit card to Shawn and said to get only what we needed. I brought my own money to get a few things for Thundering Glory. I bought a new saddle blanket, a new halter, two lead ropes and a fly mask. Then I went to see what Danny was doing.

I found him near the saddles and he was holding a dark reddish-brown one that had lots of silver trim on it.

"Wow," I said.

"Wow is right," Danny said, looking at the saddle.

"That'll be expensive here," I said quietly.

"I know, but I brought some of my own money with me," Danny said. "Shh!"

I nodded. "I can't find one that I like. Maybe I'll just wait and get one when people come to sell their horses and stuff."

"Yeah, you could probably find one," Danny said, tracing a piece of the silver with one finger. He hadn't taken his eyes off the saddle since I had gotten there.

"Well, I'm gonna go look at the show halters," I said.

Danny didn't respond.

I had a little trouble finding them, but I was happy when I did. I found a really pretty one. It was a light color with a strong headstall and a lot of silver on it. Then I went to find some new riding clothes.

All the clothes and boots were over on the opposite side of the store. I got a new pair of black jeans, a bright purple, teal and black shirt, black chaps, black boots and a black hat. I always used Wild Fire for roping and black looked really good on her. I usually make the horse and the tack I use on it contrast. If the horse is light colored, I use dark colors. If the horse is dark colored, I use light colors. It makes the horse stand out more.

"Let's go," Shawn said, holding an English saddle. "Can you take this? I gotta help Blake carry his saddles."

"Saddles?" I asked.

"Yeah. He wanted two, but don't ask me why. So he brought some of his own money to get an extra one."

"Okay," I said and took Shawn's saddle from him. I laughed as Shawn walked away, thinking to myself that we were supposed to get only what we needed. I think we all must have brought extra money. I met my brothers at the front of the store and Shawn paid for everything.

"Let's go get some stock feed and I'll buy us some burgers or something afterwards," Shawn offered as we loaded the brand new truck we had recently gotten. It wasn't to replace the one that Patrick had crashed. Shayne bought an older truck to replace that one. This one was to use to go to shows and rodeos. We used the newer trucks to pull the trailers. We had three nice, newer trucks, one older truck, and Bryson had his sport car. He was the only one that had gotten his own car yet. While Blake and Shawn spent money on their horses and other things, Jeremy and Bryson had saved up their money to buy their own cars. Jeremy was still saving up for his; he wanted a more expensive one. Patrick didn't have a chance to get his own car, and Danny and I couldn't even drive yet.

Shawn drove us out to MFA to pick up the feed Wayde had ordered, then took us to McDonalds to get some hamburgers and French fries.

On the way home, we all talked about the rodeo and the guest ranch opening up. Danny and Patrick sat in the back of the cab, while Shawn drove and Blake and I sat in the front.

"Don't we want to let Patrick drive?" Danny asked, jokingly.

Patrick punched Danny's arm as hard as he could. Danny winced and shut up.

I laughed. I was glad that Jeremy, Bryson and Shayne hadn't come along. We passed Jeremy on the highway, but he was with some of his football buddies, so he acted like he didn't know us. I stuck my tongue out at him as they drove by, but he didn't see me.

"Be nice," Shawn said.

"He didn't see me," I said.

Shawn smiled. He didn't care very much for sports either.

"How come you don't like to ride western?" I asked.

Shawn shrugged. "I dunno. I like English riding. You should try it sometime."

"I have, when I was five. Remember? Your stupid horse, Eclipse, threw me? I hate those stupid saddles."

"Yeah, but look at you now. I think getting thrown by that horse did you a lot of good. You act like you're not afraid of anything," He said. "Not even that killer horse."

"I don't think Thundering Glory meant to kill Dad," I said quietly.

"Well, personally, I don't either," Shawn admitted.

"Then why haven't you said anything?" I demanded.

"It's just such a touchy subject, I don't want to get involved," he said quietly, so that the others wouldn't hear. It didn't matter. They were off in their own little conversation and wouldn't have paid attention if we had been talking directly to them.

"So you're not taking Bryson's side?"

"I'm not taking anyone's side. I don't want to be involved. It's none of my business, and I'm keeping out of it," he said as we turned into our long driveway. The drive was about a half a mile long from the highway to the house and it was a quarter of a mile to the turn off towards the cabins.

I sighed. "Oh, all right. But I wish somebody would take my side.

"I wish there weren't sides," Shawn said, speeding up a little. I could tell He didn't want to talk anymore, so I sat back and shut my mouth.

We unloaded as soon as we got home. It was still a long time before dark, so Patrick invited Brandon and Trevin over and I invited Sarah. Then Patrick, Trevin, Brandon, Blake, Danny, Alissa, Sarah and I walked down to the pond to go swimming.

When we neared the pond, Danny ran off the dock and did a cannon ball. He came up yelling, "Cold! It's cold! Oh man it's cold!"

"Stupid!" Blake yelled at Danny as we walked out onto the dock.

"Shut up!" Danny yelled back, swimming over to the dock. "C'mon, Blake. Get in!" Danny grabbed Blake's ankle and pulled him into the pond. Blake came up and dunked Danny.

"Are we just gonna sit by and let them have all the fun or what?" Patrick asked and pulled his shirt off. He jumped in and got into the water fight.

"Woo-hoo!" Brandon yelled and jumped in.

"Ladies?" Trevin asked.

"I don't think so," Sarah said.

"Jennifer?" Trevin asked.

"What the heck?" I said and dove in. "C'mon, Alissa!"

"No way!" she called from the dock. "Too cold!"

"Suit yourself," Trevin shrugged. He dove in.

"Danny, you big baby. It ain't cold," I said.

"Is too," Danny said and splashed me.

"Hey! Stop it!" I splashed him back.

Our water fight continued, splashing people and dunking each other. Then Patrick and Brandon decided to get smart. They swam under the dock and came up near the shore.

Alissa sat on the side of the dock, her feet in the water, while Sarah had made herself comfortable on the railing. They were both facing us in the water. Patrick and Brandon quietly climbed onto the dock and over to Sarah and Alissa. Patrick nodded to Brandon and they both pushed Sarah and Alissa into the muddy water. The boys dove in after them and Patrick came up with a handful of mud. Sarah was coughing and spitting out water.

"Catch!" Patrick yelled and tossed the mud into Sarah's hair.

"You jerk!" She scraped most of it off her head and threw it at him and hit his shoulder. She went under the water and tried to rinse the thick mud out of her hair. It didn't work. "I hate you, Patrick Lee Blackwell!"

He laughed.

"It's not funny," she whined.

"Is too!" he laughed.

"You are such a jerk!" she punched his arm, then swam over next to me.

"Flirt," I whispered.

Instead of arguing, Sarah smiled.

I shook my head. "You're bad."

"I know," Sarah smiled.

Just then, Alissa screamed. "There's something on my leg!" She scrambled out of the water onto the dock.

Sure enough, stuck to her right leg was an inch long leech.

"Oh, gross!" Danny said, turning away.

"Get it off. Get it off!" Alissa begged, almost in tears.

"Calm down," Trevin said. He tried to pull it off her leg, but it hurt her and made her cry out.

"Wayde has a lighter in his truck. Let's go get it," Blake suggested, climbing out of the water.

"A lighter?" Alissa shrieked. "What for?"

"We'll have to burn it off," Blake said. He grabbed his shirt off the railing and started towards the house.

Alissa laughed nervously. "You're joking, right?"

Blake didn't answer. We followed him.

Alissa turned to me. "He is joking, right?"

"Well, that's the only way I know how to get a leach off of someone," I answered. Alissa looked so scared, I thought she was going to cry.

When we reached the truck, Blake dug around in the glove compartment, but he couldn't find a lighter. "Let's go inside."

Alissa was becoming more upset by the second. "Just get it off of me!"

"Olive do you have some matches?" Danny yelled as we walked through the door.

"Why do you need matches?" she asked, standing in the doorway to the kitchen.

"Alissa has a leech stuck, on her leg," Blake answered. "We have to burn it off."

"Oh, heavens," Olive mumbled. "C'mere. We can get it off without burning anything." Olive took Alissa's hand and led her to the bathroom. We followed behind them. I stopped to get a towel to dry off with and when I got to the bathroom, the leech was wriggling around on the linoleum.

"Danny, get rid of it," Olive said.

Danny ran to the kitchen and came back holding something in his hand.

"What is that?" Brandon asked.

"It's salt," Danny answered.

"Why in the world do you have salt?" Olive asked.

"Well, slugs melt when you put salt on them, I was wondering if leeches would do the same thing," Danny said.

Olive sighed and grabbed the salt away from Danny, then pushed past me towards the kitchen.

"Flush it down the toilet, Danny," I said and left the room. Sarah and Alissa came upstairs with me. Sarah stopped at the upstairs bathroom and took a quick shower. There were two guest bedrooms and Alissa had taken the one that Sarah wasn't using. All of the bedrooms were on the second floor, except for Grandma and Grandpa's. Shayne had the whole basement to himself. He had his bed, a refrigerator, and TV, a bathroom, and a lot of other things in the basement. He also kept his weights down there and all the boys used them. Sometimes I went down there, too, to watch and occasionally I would lift weights. But I built most of my muscles by taking care of the animals, hauling around hay bales and bags of feed.

Alissa went into her room and turned on her radio. She shut the door, but I could still hear it across the hallway to my room. I waited for Sarah to finish her shower. She went to her room to go to sleep.

Then I took a shower and went to bed. In my room, I quickly put on an old, baggy T-shirt and some shorts.

I started to comb through my hair with a pick. My hair was almost to my knees when it was wet and it took a long time to comb it all out. I usually wore it in a bun. I tried to keep it up so that it wouldn't get in my way all the time. I looked out my window. The moon cast a pale blue light across the ranch and I could see the dark shadows of the cattle out in one of the pastures.

I turned back to my room. I loved my room. It had white carpet with white walls. My curtains were white and lacy with blue trim on them that matched the canopy over my bed. My bed had a thick white and blue comforter on it with white and blue pillows. I had a fancy fan that hung in the middle of the ceiling. In one corner was a show saddle, a western one, with a lot of silver on it. There was a trophy on the floor next to it. On one wall was a shelf that held trophies and ribbons that I had won over the years.

I stretched and crawled into bed. I fell asleep almost as soon as my head hit the pillow.

Chapter 12

Selling Thundering Glory

The next morning, Angie woke me up at 7:30 sharp, which made me angry. I don't like to get up early if I don't get a lot of sleep or if I worked hard the day before. I lay in bed and pulled the blanket over my head.

A few minutes later, Angie ran back in and jumped on me, talking a million miles an hour about something that I didn't understand.

"... And they're coming to pick him up in a couple of minutes."

I sat up sleepily. "Pick who up?" I asked.

Angie sighed exasperatedly. "I just told you. The Johnsons are coming to buy Thundering Glory."

"What?" I shrieked. I jumped out of bed, knocking Angie off the bed, and got dressed as quickly

as I could. The whole time I kept thinking about how mean the Johnson boys were to their animals. They mistreated them and rarely fed them right. They beat their horses when they rode them and sometimes they beat them just for fun. I couldn't believe that Wayde and Grandpa would sell Thundering Glory to them!

I ran past Sarah and Alissa in the hallway and ran down the stairs, then outside.

The Johnsons were already there, waiting by the trailer. The two younger boys were anyway. There were three boys. Zach at ten was ten youngest, Jonah was thirteen and Skyler was fifteen. I couldn't stand them. I hardly knew Skyler, even though we went to school together, but he seemed to be the nicest one. He was quiet and stuck up. The other two were loud and rude. I couldn't decide which was worse.

Jonah grinned when he saw me. "I hear you don't wanna sell the horse that killed your pa."

"I'm not selling my horse," I corrected him.

"We're gonna break that horse for rodeos," he said.

"You're not even gonna touch my horse!" I angrily yelled at him.

Wayde came out of the barn, leading Thundering Glory. As soon as he saw me, Thundering Glory reared up and whinnied. Wayde tried to calm him down, but to no avail. The powerful horse reared on his hind legs over and over, pawing at the air with his hooves.

Jonah laughed, "That idiot's gonna get himself killed, just like your pa did."

Jonah's remark made me so angry that, without even thinking, I spun around on my heels and punched him. He yelped and bent over, holding his eye.

I walked over to where Thundering Glory was and grabbed the lead rope from Wayde. "Easy, boy, easy," I said quietly. Thundering Glory stood still. "Good boy, good boy." I stroked his nose.

I think Wayde was in shock at first, but then he smiled. However, Mr. Johnson, I could tell, was not impressed. He hastily took the lead away from me and started to lead Thundering Glory over to the trailer where Jonah stood, still holding his eye.

"Jonah, open that door," Mr. Johnson barked.

Obediently, Jonah opened the door.

"No!" I protested.

"Jennifer, don't," Grandma said.

"He's my horse and you can't have him!" I yelled.

"Not again with the 'it's my horse' stuff," Shayne rolled his eyes. "We can not keep such a dangerous animal around here with the ranch opening. If anyone got hurt, we'd be sued for sure. Then they'd kill him. Do you really want that?"

I turned to Grandpa. "Please, please don't let them have him. They won't treat him right!"

"We can't keep him, I'm sorry, honey," Grandpa said.

I felt tears welling up inside and I swallowed to keep from crying. "You can't sell him," I said quietly.

Zach was in the trailer, pulling on the lead rope. Thundering Glory had his feet planted and wasn't budging an inch. Mr. Johnson got angry and went to his truck. He returned holding a lunge line whip.

"No!" I ran over and tried to pull the whip away from him. "Don't hit him!"

"Get away from me!" Mr. Johnson shoved me to the ground, then whipped Thundering Glory until he was in the trailer. Skyler had gotten out of the truck just in time to see what had just happened.

"Now you just wait a minute," Wayde spoke up.

Everyone looked at him. I stayed on the ground, sitting on the sharp gravel. My palms were scraped, but I didn't notice them, even though they were stinging and my right hand still had a rock stuck in it.

"This little girl has done everything in her power to keep that horse from harm. She loves that horse, and we all know it. We all also know he will not be cared for at the Johnson's stable," Wayde said.

"Now you just wait a second there, cowboy," Mr. Johnson said. "I don't know just who you think you are, but-"

"I'm a close friend of this family, and I'm not about to sit by and let you take away the only thing she has left from her father." Turning to Grandpa, Wayde said, "I don't know what Mr. Johnson's paying you for that horse, but whatever it is, I'll double it."

"Well, now, Wayde, that's quite a bit of money. Are you sure?" Grandpa asked after a minute of thinking.

Wayde nodded.

Skyler walked over and offered me a hand to help me up. "Are you all right?"

"Yeah," I mumbled. I pulled the small rock out of my hand, then brushed the dust off of my denim shorts.

"Well, I'm sorry, Mr. Johnson, but it looks like you'll have to find yourself another horse somewhere else," Grandpa said.

"Wait a minute, Henry. Now I thought we had a deal. I paid you for that horse and I'm not sellin'. You've got the check right there in your pocket," Mr. Johnson said.

"I have the check," Grandpa said, taking it out of his pocket, "But nothing's been cashed yet. So..." Grandpa tore the check up and handed the pieces to Mr. Johnson. "Unload that horse, Mr. Johnson. It belongs to my granddaughter."

Shayne's jaw hung open. "You can't let her keep that horse!"

Grandpa ignored Shayne. "Unload him."

Mr. Johnson was angry and for a minute, I thought another fight was going to break out. But then Mr. Johnson said, "Jonah, unload that animal."

"But, Pa-" Jonah started.

"Just do what I tell you, boy!"

Jonah stood still, pouting like a three-year-old.

"Skyler! Get that horse out of the trailer," Mr. Johnson ordered.

Skyler seemed happy to do it. He backed Thundering Glory out of the trailer and handed the lead rope to me. I decided then that maybe I had misjudged Skyler. I had been right about the rest of them though.

Thundering Glory seemed happy too. He threw his head up and down and nipped at my shirtsleeve. I stroked his nose.

Mr. Johnson hastily loaded his boys into his truck and drove off so quickly his tires squealed and gravel was thrown at least four feet into the air.

"Thank you so much, Wayde," I said and threw my arms around his neck.

"You're welcome, sweetie. Your horse will be much happier here than with them. He's your horse now. No one can touch him. He's yours," Wayde said.

"Well, you'd better get to working with him if you ever want to ride him. You and Wayde take him down to the arena and I'll be down there as soon as I change these clothes," Grandpa said.

I smiled.

"Don't stand there, take that horse down to the arena," Grandpa ordered.

"Yes, sir," I said happily and led Thundering Glory down to the arena with Wayde following behind me.

"We've really got our work cut out for us with this one," Wayde said as he opened the gate for me. "I don't even know where to begin."

Alissa came out of the tack shed, carrying the English saddle and a bridle.

"I think it's a little early to be putting a saddle on him, don't you?" Grandpa called, walking down to the arena with Patrick. They walked through the gate, then closed it behind them.

I smiled at Alissa. She smiled back and started to giggle.

"Uh-oh," Patrick laughed.

"I know that look," Wayde said. "Your granddaughter's got something up her sleeve, Henry."

"Jenny's always got something up her sleeve," Patrick said. "That's my Baby Sis!"

Alissa laughed and put the saddle blanket on Thundering Glory's back. I put the saddle on him and cinched it up. Then I put the bridle on as Grandpa, Patrick and Wayde watched. I untied Thundering Glory from the post and led him over to where they were standing.

Wayde smiled and shook his head. "I should have known. So this was the reason you were getting up at 4:30 in the morning."

I shrugged.

"Well, get on and let me see how he rides," Grandpa said.

"Well..." I started.

"Well, what?" Grandpa asked.

"I haven't rode him yet. I'm too nervous," I answered.

"My sister? Scared of a horse? Since when?" Patrick demanded.

"It's not like that," I said. "I didn't want everyone to know that we were breaking him. If I got hurt, you would have sold him for sure. But now that you know, I'll try to ride him. Just hold on to him for me."

Patrick held the reins as I mounted as quickly as I could. As soon as Patrick let go of the reins, Thundering Glory took off at a full gallop. Then he suddenly ducked his head and I knew what was coming. He stopped and threw me over his head to the hard ground. All the air was forced out of my lungs. I laid there, gasping for air, expecting Thundering Glory to step on me, but he stood still, nudging my shoulder with his nose. I slowly stood back up.

"Are you all right?" Wayde called.

"Ouch!" I jokingly called back.

"Try it again!" Grandpa yelled.

I took the reins and put them back over Thundering Glory's neck, swearing to myself that I wouldn't have gotten thrown if I had decided to use a western saddle instead. "I hate English saddles!" I yelled.

"English saddles rock!" Came Shawn's voice from the opposite side of the arena.

I looked and saw him standing next to Patrick, his elbow on Alissa's shoulder as if she were an armrest. Then I pulled Thundering Glory's head around to where he could see what I was doing. I mounted up and he reared before I could get my right foot in the stirrup. I landed, not quite as painfully this time, in the dirt of the arena. For one thing, I was not wearing the right clothes to be riding. Shorts and sneakers don't go with unbroken horses. Shoot, shorts and sneakers don't go with any horse, period. I repeatedly got back on as quickly as I could, and each time he threw me. Some of the time I barely got half way on and he would rare up, other times I would get on, and he would buck. I was soon sore and bruised. I was back near the gate and Patrick and Shawn were laughing at me. I was aching all over.

"Can somebody else do this, please?" I asked, exhaustedly.

Grandpa shook his head. "This is your horse, you need to do it. Do it again."

I groaned and tried again, but I was thrown. "What am I doing wrong?" I asked, sitting on the ground, Thundering Glory swishing his tail at flies and hitting me in the process.

"You kick him in the side every time you mount," Patrick laughed.

"Is that all?" I asked.

Wayde nodded.

"And you knew this the whole time I was being mutilated?" I demanded.

"Um, maybe?" Shawn answered, trying not to laugh.

I could have broken both of their necks. I was careful not to kick Thundering Glory in his side as I mounted. He stood still and turned his head to look at me. It almost seemed that he was laughing at me too. "Oh, shut up," I mumbled.

Wayde attached a lungeline to Thundering Glory's bridle and got him to walk in a circle.

"Make him trot," I said. I was having so much fun.

Thundering Glory speeded up to a quick trot. To my surprise, his gate was smooth.

"Too fast?" Wayde asked.

"No," I answered. "He's got a smooth gate."

We lunged him for about twenty minutes, getting him used to me on his back. Then Wayde stopped him. "Let's walk him around and let you do some riding, not lunging. I'll have control of him, but I'm gonna let you teach him."

"Okay," I said nervously. My heart was pounding and my hands were shaking, but I forced my legs to relax so Thundering Glory wouldn't know I was nervous. I squeezed my legs together, making him walk. I pulled on the left rein and he turned left. I pulled on the right rein and he turned right. He acted the way a well-broken horse would, not like a horse that was just being broken. Dangerous? Shayne was wrong.

Chapter 13

Getting Ready to Open

Every morning and every evening I worked with Wayde and Alissa, breaking Thundering Glory. But I was the only one he would let ride him. He threw Wayde and would almost sit down and make Alissa slide off backwards. It seemed like he didn't want to hurt Alissa (I knew he didn't) but he didn't want her riding him. I could ride him all I wanted. I was surprised, as was everyone else, that he learned so quickly. I couldn't believe how lucky I was.

He liked trail rides and behaved fairly well on them when I went riding with my brothers. He was pretty jumpy, though, because he was still only green broke. He would bolt if there was a strange sound or if something crossed the trail, but he did well for only being green broke. If I didn't take him out riding, or at least let him out of his stall, he would kick the walls of his stall and make a terrible racket until I came to see him.

Danny tried to ride him, which was about the dumbest thing he had done in a long time. It was almost like a bronco ride, Danny got thrown around so much. It was funny, though, because I had just told Danny he would get thrown. He ignored me, of course, and really got a ride. He didn't try to ride him after that. When I jokingly asked him why, he told me to shut up.

One day, Blake woke me up at four in the morning.

"Gotta get ready," he said.

"For what?" I asked, yawning.

"Remember? Today is the opening day!" he answered and left the room.

I jumped out of bed. "Yes!"

Max, who had been sleeping on the floor beside my bed, jumped up, barking.

"Max, Shh!" I ran to my closet and got dressed as quickly as I could. Max made himself comfortable on my bed as I dressed. I put on some old, torn up jeans, a T-shirt and my old boots. I ran down to the kitchen with Max in tow, grabbed two apples, then ran out to the barn. I gave one of the apples to Thundering Glory and ate the other one myself as I fed and watered the horses.

Grandpa appeared in the doorway. "As soon as you can, start saddling those horses. I'll send Blake and Shayne out to take them over to the trail corral. Do you want to be a trail guide?"

"Sure!" I leaped at the chance to be a trail guide. I usually just signed everyone up for trail rides. But I rode the trails so much, I knew them like the back of my hand. I knew which ones were the longer ones, which ones were the most rocky, which ones had the most hills and, if small children were riding, which trail would be the safest for them to ride.

"You can do that this afternoon," Grandpa said and left.

I started saddling horses. I had already saddled six horses and was saddling Firefly, one of Blake's horses, when Patrick and Danny came to take the horses over to the corral. They saddled Degenerate and Double J, mounted up and led the other horses to the corral. We usually had about ten to twelve horses for the guests to ride and two horses for each of us. That way, we could give the horses a break between each ride.

I saddled six more horses and then saddled Take-Time to take them over to the corral. It was about a twenty-minute ride, walking the horses, so I settled back to relax. I would have gone faster, but leading all those horses, I decided it might be dangerous, so I took it slow.

"There she is," Wayde said when I neared the corral.

"Waiting on me?" I asked.

"We were just getting ready to come get the horses," Danny said as he took them from me.

"Uh-huh. Sure you were," I teased, dismounting. "What time will everyone start coming?"

"Seven," Patrick yawned.

I yawned to. "You made me yawn," I said and lightly hit him.

He shrugged. "Can't help it."

I looked at my watch. It read 5:37.

"Danny," Wayde said. "I want you and Jennifer to take Double J, ride over to the guest stables and open all the stalls. "

Danny smiled at me. "C'mon, Jenn."

I mounted Double J, then slid behind the saddle as Danny got on.

"Don't you two go doing anything stupid," Wayde said.

"Okay," Danny said and nudged the horse into a trot.

I held onto my brother's shoulders and Double J trotted along.

"He sure has a rough gate, doesn't he?" I asked.

"Kind'a," Danny answered. "It's just because you're on the back."

"I suppose. I'm getting bored back here. Let's go," I said.

"You wanna run?" Danny asked.

"That's what I just said," I answered.

"I wasn't talking to you," he said. "All right Double J. Let's show Baby Sis what you can do." I held on tighter to Danny's shoulders and he kicked Double J. The horse took off and Danny let him go as fast as he wanted. I loved to race on horses. Danny laughed. "You can do better than this," he said and kicked Double J again. The horse ran even faster. It only took us about five minutes to get to the barn. Danny tied Double J up to let him eat, then we went inside the barn.

We started opening the stall doors and putting the numbers on the doors, so that people would know which stalls they had reserved for their horses.

"I can't wait for everyone to get here," Danny said.

"I know, me either," I answered.

"I can't believe they let you keep Thundering Glory. He's really special to you, isn't he?"

"Yeah."

You gonna enter him in the rodeo?"

"I dunno."

"You should."

"Why?"

"He's fast. You'd win the barrel races for sure," Danny said as he slid a door open. It squeaked as it opened and hurt my ears.

"I haven't practiced barrel racing with him. He might spook. Besides, I use Take-Time for barrel racing."

"Then race him for something."

"You and your racing. Are you going to race Double J?"

"Yep. Well, that's done. Let's get the other barn opened up," Danny said and started for the doorway. I followed.

We opened the stalls in the other barn, mounted Double J and rode back to the house. Danny made Double J walk so I could rest. I tried to stay awake, but my head kept nodding, so I rested my head on the back of Danny's shoulder and fell asleep.

Danny woke me up as we entered the driveway to the house. "You'd better saddle a horse. I'll see you later."

"All right," I said and slid backwards off of Double J.

"Don't do that! You're gonna get kicked in the head one of these days," Danny warned.

"Aw, you worry too much," I said and slapped Double J. He cantered away.

"Get dressed," Jeremy said, coming out of the house with Bryson.

"What do you care?" I asked.

Jeremy shrugged. "Just thought you might want to look nice." They started for Bryson's car. When he reached the door, he turned back to me. "Oh, and I'd keep Thundering...whatever out of sight. If people find out about him, it'd be bad for business." With that, they got in the car and drove off.

I rolled my eyes, but decided it was a good idea after all. People wouldn't go trail riding if they thought our horses were mean or uncontrollable. I went to my room. I put on nice blue jeans, my new black boots, black chaps, a small, nice, white T-shirt, and my black hat. Then I headed back to the stable.

Wild Fire was a bright reddish-brown 7-year-old Thoroughbred mare. She was tall and fast. I decided Thoroughbreds were becoming my favorite horses instead of Quarter Horses. Wild Fire's front legs and right back leg had white stockings and she had a white blaze on her face. Her black mane was short and neatly brushed to the right side of her neck. She had a long, black tail. I saddled her with a lot of fancy tack, just to show off. I put on my spurs, then rode to the front entrance. By that time it was 6:45.

Grandpa had hired extra help for the ranch. That was usually Dad's job, but Grandpa had to take over it. One of the hired hands was at the front gate.

"You must be Mr. Blackwell's granddaughter," she said when she saw me.

"Yeah," I said and rode over to where she was. She sat in a small booth, almost like pay tolls along the highway. She was in charge of checking everyone into the ranch.

"I'm Sharon," She smiled. She had long, wavy brown hair and brown eyes. She was wearing a red shirt and a brown cowboy hat. "Will you be riding in the rodeo?"

"Uh-huh. You?" I asked.

"Yeah, a little. I don't know, I might be too busy, though, with other things. Your grandpa sure has a lot of things for us to do around here," Sharon said.

"Um, yeah. Usually my Dad is in charge around here and things get done quicker," I said.

"Why didn't he do it this year?" she asked.

"He passed away about a month ago," I answered, looking towards the highway. I expected her to start with the "I'm so sorries", but she didn't.

"You and your Dad were close, weren't you?" she asked.

"Yeah."

"And you're upset because he left you."

I nodded.

"Ya know, I lost my dad when I was about your age."

"Really?" I turned to look at her. "If you don't mind my asking, what happened?"

"He was killed in a rodeo, bull riding. I was thirteen and I saw the whole thing. I was really hurt. I hated the bull and I couldn't even stand to look at a cow without getting this sick feeling in my stomach," Sharon said. Then she laughed. "Every time I ate a hamburger I went out near the pasture where we kept our cattle."

I laughed. "Did you really?"

"Yeah. I really did. Like the cows really cared anyway," she looked at me. "But then, my mother wanted to sell the animals and move to the city. I wasn't mad at the animals anymore. I realized they're just animals and the don't understand things the way we do. They can't reason. They go on instincts. The bull didn't mean to kill my father, it was just a natural reaction for it to throw a person off of its back."

"Did your mother sell the animals?" I asked.

"No, a friend talked her out of it. I took lessons about how to ride and now I'm not afraid of the animals anymore," Sharon said.

I thought about what she had just said. "Thanks, but it's not me that's angry at the horse who killed my dad, it's my brothers Shayne and Bryson. But thanks. I don't feel so alone anymore."

Sharon nodded. "If you ever need to talk, I'm right here." Then looking towards the road we saw three trucks with trailers pulling in to our turn off.

"Get ready," I warned, "You've got a long day ahead of you." I bumped Wild Fire's sides and trotted her a little way down the drive to where Danny and Blake sat on their horses, waiting.

Chapter 14

The Rodeo

By ten o'clock, everyone was settled in and Grandpa called all the people into the dining room. The hall was a tall, long building with rafters and ceiling fans. There were tables in four rows and a kitchen behind them. At the side of the dining hall was a stage where announcements were made. Sometimes after rodeos they would clear out all the tables and have a dance. They would call a small town band that played country music, wanting to make a little money, to perform. Or my brothers and I would sing. Like I said earlier, Shayne likes to sing and has a really good voice.

Grandpa stood proud and tall on the stage. He cleared his throat and began to give his opening speech.

"First of all, I would like to thank you all for coming out here to spend a weekend, a week, or longer at the Shining Star Ranch. I am the owner, Mr. Henry L. Blackwell. My family and I have spent weeks preparing for your arrival and have worked long and hard. We would appreciate it if you would treat the property and animals as if they were your own. Some of you have been here before, I recognize a few of your faces, and we would like to welcome you back. To those of you who are new, welcome, we hope you enjoy your stay."

"It's the exact same speech every year," Sarah whispered to me. I tried not to giggle.

"I know," I whispered back. "Oh well. That's Grandpa for you. I think he just keeps the paper in his dresser drawer and gets it out every year."

"Now I would like to introduce the faculty who work here. I'll let my granddaughter do that. Jennifer, would you please come up here?" Grandpa invited me up on stage.

I was excited; I'd never spoken at the opening meeting before. I was also very nervous. Danny had done it the year before and had introduced everyone. He messed up a little and I teased him for a week. I just knew he was going to get me back if I messed up. I walked up on stage as everyone politely applauded.

"Thanks," I started. "Well, as Grandpa said, I am Jennifer Blackwell, and I am one of the trail guides this year. I'm going to introduce everyone that will be working here so that you kind'a get to know them. First is my brother Danny and he is also a trail guide..."

Danny stood up briefly then quickly sat down and slouched in his seat.

I went on to introduce everyone, then Shayne came up on stage to announce some of the rules and regulations. He also announced the rodeo and livestock shows.

After everyone was dismissed, I found Danny, Patrick and Trevin waiting for me.

"You just had to introduce me first, didn't you?" Danny demanded.

I smiled at him. "Yup. Sure did."

"I'm gonna kill you," he said with a smile.

"I'm waiting."

"Hey, Patrick said I could help out with the trail rides," Trevin announced.

"You two are going to be tour guides together? Man, get ready for some dead riders and injured horses," I said.

"Shut up," Trevin mumbled.

"Let's go. We'd better go before the guests get there," Patrick said. He and Trevin ran over to Trevin's old beat up '87 Chevy truck and peeled out, heading for the trail corral.

"That is the ugliest truck I have ever seen in my life," Danny said, shaking his head as the truck drove away.

I laughed. "Let's go."

We walked over to where Double J and Wild Fire were, mounted and rode up to the trail corral. Patrick, Blake and Trevin were waiting for us.

"We need customers, we need customers," Blake sing-songed.

Soon a van pulled up and four little kids got out.

"I wanna ride the biggest horse!" the little boy cried.

"Now just wait a second," his mother said, getting out of the van. "We don't know the age limit. Are these horses safe?"

"Of course they're safe," the father answered. "They wouldn't have trail riding if they weren't safe."

"I assure you, ma'am, these horses are the gentlest horses in Randolph County," Blake said, standing up straight. I tried not to laugh at him.

"Besides, Jennifer over there knows these trails like the back of her hand. She rides them all the time," Trevin put in.

About that time a bright red mustang pulled up. No one seemed to notice until Jeremy stuck his head out and yelled, "Yo! Patrick!"

"No way!" Patrick exclaimed and ran over to the car.

"Are you sure?" the mother asked the father.

"Honey, don't worry so much. Where do I pay?" he asked.

"Right over there, sir," Trevin answered. The man went to the small store a little way up the hill to pay. By this time, there were several cars that had pulled in.

I helped six children on horses, told them how make the horses stop and go, then started to lead them out on the trail.

We worked hard for those two weeks before the rodeo. We got up every morning before daylight to get ready for the day ahead. Then, after many long days, it was finally the day of the rodeo. You could just feel the excitement in the air. It was so thick you could cut it with a knife. There were a lot of horses everywhere, people running about and causing a lot of commotion.

Before the rodeo began, I was getting ready too; my first event was steer wrestling. Not very many females entered those kind of events, but I liked them. There was a knock at the door and I let Patrick in.

"I've got some bad news, Jenn," Patrick said.

"What's happened now?" I asked, looking in the mirror to make sure I looked all right.

"You know Sky Lark?" He asked.

"Yeah, the horse I use to steer wrestle. What about her?"

"She's gone lame. You'll have to sit out the steer wrestling this time."

"What?" I spun around to look at my brother.

Patrick shrugged. "Sorry, Jenny."

I sighed. "That's not fair."

"Maybe you could use another horse," Patrick though aloud.

"Yeah, right. Which horse?"

"Well..." Patrick started.

Just then Blake came in the room.

"No! N-O. Big no-no. Patrick I can't! My butt will be so grounded! I can't. No way."

"What's up?" Blake asked.

"Sky Lark went lame. Jenny needs a new horse to steer wrestle with," Patrick answered.

"So?" Blake asked.

"Let me spell it out for you. N-O-W-A-Y!" I insisted.

"Oh," Blake said. He and Patrick smiled at each other, then took me by the upper arms and drug me outside and into the barn.

"Here," Patrick said, "Is your steer wrestling horse."

"Thundering Glory hasn't been used for steer wrestling! I refuse!" I yelled at them.

"It's this or nothing," Blake said with a shrug.

"But, I just-"

"Just wanna win this year?" Patrick finished my sentence.

"Yeah," I said.

"Good."

"But, Patrick-"

"Saddle up." He clapped me on the back and he and Blake left the barn.

"Why do I always get talked into things?" I asked Thundering Glory as I led him out of his stall.

I tied him to a post and started to brush him down. "You're gonna be good for me, right?" I asked him. "You're not gonna throw me are you?" I got out a saddle and put it on his back. I continued to talk to him the whole time I was saddling him. Then I mounted and slowly rode over to the large arena.

I heard music in the distance. Before the rodeo began they would usually let Blake and Danny play loud music. They usually played Garth Brooks, because that's what most people at the rodeos like. But now they were being annoying and were playing "Mmm-Bop" by Hanson. The music got louder as we got closer and Thundering Glory picked up his ears and looked around nervously. I could feel him tensing up beneath me, but I gave him some encouragement and urged him to trot. I rode around behind the pens to see if there was anyone I recognized from the years before. I didn't see anyone, so I stayed there, waiting for the rodeo to start.

"Hey, aren't you that chick that was talking at the main hall a few days ago?" a boy asked as he rode over towards me. He looked about my age; he had a black cowboy hat that covered his hair, bright blue eyes and a dark blue shirt.

"Uh, yeah. My name's Jennifer. What's yours? Don't call me 'chick'. I hate that," I said.

"Sorry. My name's Christian and this is Tex," he explained in a heavy southern accent. He petted the dark brown and white paint he was riding.

"Where are you from?" I asked.

"Arkansas. What's your horse's name?"

"Thundering Glory."

"Is it yours?"

"Yep."

"Man, I'd sure like to own a horse like that. You think maybe I could ride him sometime?"

"No," I answered bluntly.

"How come?" Christian asked. "I'm real good with horses."

"So is the rest of my family. But that doesn't mean they can ride my horse."

Christian didn't say anything and I began to feel guilty.

"It's not like I won't let them, he just throws everyone but me," I finally said.

"Oh. Do you have any more horses of your own?" he asked.

"Seven, counting this one."

"Really?" he seemed impressed. "This is my only horse. Well, besides a little pony I have, but I'm going to sell it."

"I like your horse," I said.

"Thanks. I gucss it's timc to start. Do you go first?"

"No, I'm fourth. I got lucky. I ain't the first and I ain't the last."

"I'm second. How come steer wrestling is first?"

"I dunno," I sighed. "My brother's in charge this year instead of my Dad."

"How come?" Christian asked.

I didn't want to talk about it, so I changed the subject. "You're just full of questions, aren't you? Why do you have to be so nosy?"

The first person prepared to start the event. I couldn't help being nervous. I forced my self to relax again. It's hard to do. Thundering Glory was getting nervous also. He was pawing at the ground and kept biting the bit. My hands were shaking. I was beginning to have second thoughts about using Thundering Glory and just when I had about decided to change my mind and back out, my name was called and I didn't have a choice. I was becoming more nervous by the second and at one point I though I was going to be sick. I rode into the arena and got to my starting place. The rodeo clowns were walking around near the center of the arena. I laughed nervously when one of them pointed at me and jokingly slid his finger across his throat. They always teased me like that. Only this time I really didn't think it was funny. I searched the crowd for familiar faces. I saw Sarah, Alissa, and a few friends from school. I took one last breath before the buzzer sounded and the steer bolted out of the pen.

I kicked Thundering Glory and he took off faster than what I was used to. He came up next to the steer quickly and I got ready to go. I took my left foot over the stirrup, crossed it over as quickly as I could to the right side, and the rest is a blur. As I jumped I knew something was wrong. I saw the steer, but I didn't get a hold of its horns. I landed on the ground and then everything went black.

Chapter 15

A Visit to the Hospital

I woke up in a room I didn't recognize. The walls were white and it was really quiet. The air was cold and I couldn't figure out where I was. I looked around for something familiar and saw Danny.

"Danny?" I asked quietly.

He looked up and smiled suddenly. "You're awake."

"Yeah. Where in the heck am I?"

"You're in the hospital. You hit your head and the steer stepped on you. You've been out cold for the past four hours," he answered.

"Four hours?" I tried to sit up, but I got dizzy and fell back. "What time is it?"

"11:45. Do you feel okay?"

"My head hurts and my ribs. And my arm. My arm hurts." I noticed my arm was in a sling.

Just then the doctor walked in the room with Grandpa and Wayde. "You're up," the doctor smiled. "About time, young lady, you gave everyone quite a scare."

"Can I go home?" I asked sleepily.

"Not so fast" The doctor held up a hand. "Mr. Blackwell, your granddaughter is very lucky, as far as the bump on her head. She has a slight concussion, but her arm is broken and she has some bruised ribs. I want to keep her here for a little while and then she can go home."

Danny sighed.

"I don't want to stay here!" I protested. "I hate hospitals."

"We'll put her arm in a cast tomorrow. See you in the morning, Jennifer," the doctor said and left the room.

"We've got to be gettin' home, young 'un. We'll be back tomorrow," Wayde said.

"You're just going to leave me?"

"We can't stay. You'll be fine," Grandpa explained, then he, Wayde and Danny left the hospital.

I can't believe them! I thought to myself. I tried to go to sleep, but I couldn't. I tried to roll over on my right side, but it made my ribs hurt. I tried to lay on my left side, but I accidentally laid on my broken arm and made it hurt worse. I finally just laid flat on my back and stared at the ceiling. Eventually, I fell asleep.

A nurse woke me up in the morning to put my arm in a cast. I had had casts before and I hated them. They itched and got in the way all the time. I couldn't stand them. They offered to make the cast colored, like blue or green, but I told them no. It was embarrassing enough just being white. I had to eat the food, which was terrible, and my room smelled of medicine. After lunch, Shayne, Patrick, Blake and Bryson came to see me.

"How ya' doin' kid?" Shayne asked.

"What do you think?" I asked jokingly.

"Ooh! I get to sign your cast first!" Blake exclaimed and ran over. He got a thin black marker and wrote, "Smile! Love Blake," on it. Each of my brothers wrote something on my cast. The funniest was Bryson's message. He wrote, "I told you so ~ Bryson."

I about died laughing. He told me he was serious, but I laughed anyway.

Sarah and Alissa came in later with two of our friends from school, Walt and Josh. Josh was Sarah's boyfriend at the time. He was wearing a white T-shirt with a red jersey over it and a red baseball cap. He was about Sarah's height and was really quiet. He laughed a lot and smiled all the time. I thought they were a cute couple.

Walt was tall and slender with light brown hair and blue eyes. He put wax in his hair to make it stand up. He was wearing his yellow coat and blue jeans.

Josh read what my brothers had written, laughed then signed his name. "Having fun?"

"Shut up," I mumbled.

"I brought something that will cheer you up," Sarah smiled. She got a picture out of her backpack and stuck it on the wall with tacky-glue. The picture was a cat with the word "Wow!" under it. The cat's eyes were big and its mouth was open in a big "O". I laughed and I was immediately sorry I did. My ribs ached when I laughed, but it felt good to have people trying to cheer me up. Then Sarah wrote on my cast. She wrote, "One word, Unkpute! L.Y.L.A.S. Sarah." Then she laughed at her own cleverness. L.Y.L.A.S. stands for, Love Ya Like A Sister. We never knew what an unkpute was or what it stood for. It was just something we heard on TV one day. We could just say the word "Unkpute" and we would both burst out laughing. We never knew why.

"You're an idiot," Walt laughed and signed his name. "When are you coming home?"

"Tomorrow," I answered.

"Well, this certainly isn't a first," Alissa said. "I hear you've been here before."

"You all leave me alone! You're so mean to me!" I fake-sobbed.

"Oh, yes. We are just so cruel, aren't we?" Sarah jokingly yelled back.

"You are!"

"Okay, we'll just leave then," Walt said and started towards the door.

"No! Stay! Don't leave me here. They torture me!" I exclaimed.

"Okay, I guess we'll stay here and protect you," Walt sighed then laughed.

"We got you something," Alissa said. She reached in Sarah's backpack and pulled out a fairly large present and placed in on my bed.

I sat up and started opening it. "What'd you get me?" Inside of the present was another present. I opened five presents, each inside of the other, until I got to the actual present. I gasped when I saw it. "Garth Brooks 'Seven'! I love you guys!" I held the new C.D. in my hands and stared at it. They had forgotten to take the price tag off. It said *SALE $14.96.*

Sarah smiled. "Now you'll quit taking mine!"

A nurse came in and told them they had to leave before I could thank them again. I didn't have a C.D. player, so I just opened the cover and stared at the pictures on the inside cover and read the lyrics. Later that afternoon, Patrick, Brandon and Trevin came by to see me. Brandon grabbed the C.D. away from me and looked at it. Then he began to sing in a high and off-pitch voice, "Everybody! Yeah, rock your body! Yeah!"

"Shut up," I mumbled. "You're not funny. You're just stupid."

"Backstreet Boys rule!" he cried in a high-pitched voice.

"Not really. Any one of them could probably take you anyway."

"Yeah, right."

"They probably could," Trevin laughed.

"Whose side are you on?" Brandon demanded.

"It depends. Are you arguing with Jennifer or fighting with a member of a boy-band?" Trevin asked.

"Arguing with Jennifer," Brandon said.

"Okay, then I'm on Jennifer's side."

"Then I'm fighting with what's-his-face in a boy-band."

"Then I'm on what's-his-face's side."

Patrick laughed out loud. Brandon hit Trevin, but Trevin didn't even flinch.

"I like Garth Brooks and Tim McGraw better anyway," I said.

"Can I sign your cast?" Trevin asked.

"I guess," I shrugged.

"All righty," He walked over and grabbed a marker off the tabletop. He scribbled his name on my cast. "There. Now your arm is famous."

"Just because you signed it?" I asked.

"Yep."

"Okay then," I laughed and rolled my eyes.

"You doin' all right?" Patrick asked.

"Considering my ribs are all busted up, my arm's in a cast and I'm in a hospital, yeah, I guess I'm doin' all right," I answered.

"Well, we gotta go. We'll come get you tomorrow," Patrick said.

"Come first thing in the morning!" I called after them.

"All right," Patrick waved and they left.

I laid back and stared at the pictures on the C.D.

I was happy to get home, but they wouldn't let me do anything. They didn't want me to ride horses (I really didn't want to because of my ribs), much less be a trail guide; I couldn't go swimming or help out with the ranch at all. I stayed inside most of the time, helping Olive.

"It's not fair, Olive," I complained while I was cutting up lettuce for salad.

"Well, sometimes life's not fair," she said, looking at a cookbook.

I put the lettuce in a large wooden bowl. "I can't do anything and this stupid cast keeps getting in my way!" I exclaimed, scratching at the cast on my arm. It was big and bulky and was just plain annoying. I hated it.

"Hmm," Olive continued to stare at the book.

"You're not even listening to me are you?"

"Hmm."

I decided I'd have a little fun and see how long it took Olive to catch on to what I was saying. "And, um, so anyway, Grandpa said he'd take me to get a new car of my own."

"Mmm-hmm."

"And he'd just take the money out of your paycheck..."

"That's nice. Where did I put that garlic?" Olive thought aloud.

"And I was abducted by aliens last night. They had these great big needles and I think they must have tagged me or something because this is like the fourth time it's happened. They must have put something on my brain because I keep twitching and it won't stop..."

"Yep. Oh there it is!" Olive exclaimed and reached into the cabinet.

"So can I go ride with Patrick and them?" I asked.

"Uh-huh," Olive nodded.

"Thanks!" I said and left the kitchen.

"Wait, uh, Jennifer?" Olive called after me.

I pretended I didn't hear her. I walked towards the guest part of the ranch because no one was near our house. I finally reached the guest part of the ranch, but I didn't see anyone I knew. Until I heard a voice from behind me yell, "Hey, Jennifer!" I turned around and saw Christian on Tex. "What are ya doin'?"

"Walking," I replied dully.

"I'm just ridin' around. Haven't seen you since that steer tore you up. You feelin' okay?" he asked.

"My ribs are busted and so is my arm. Do you think I'm okay?" I snapped.

"Sorry," he said. He really looked hurt again.

"I'm okay," I sighed.

"I'm glad to hear it," he said, looking towards the road. "I don't suppose you'd want to ride with me?"

I didn't answer for a long time. I decided I didn't want to hurt his feeling for yet a third time, so I said, "For a little while."

"Hop on," he smiled and took his foot out of the stirrup.

I went to mount and there was a sharp stab in my side. "Oh!" I cried.

"Here, let me help," Christian reached down and took my hand. He pulled me up behind him and asked, "Where to?"

"I don't care, just take it slow," I said.

"All right," he agreed and made Tex walk. We rode along some trails and beside the highway. I was glad to get to ride again, but for some reason I felt like I shouldn't have been with Christian. I didn't know why. He liked me, I could tell he did, and he looked good. But for some reason I didn't like him back. He was sweet and sincere, but all I ever did was snap at him. I was attempting to figure it out as we rode along. "Can we go look at your horses?"

"I guess," I said. "Do you know where the barn is?"

"Isn't it towards your house?" he asked.

"Yeah."

"Good. Now I get to see where you live."

We rode along the drive towards the house. When we got closer, and the house was visible, Christian exclaimed, "That's your house?"

"Yeah, why?" I asked.

"It's huge!"

"It ain't that big," I said.

"It's nice looking."

"Thank you." I was proud of myself. I was already being nicer to him.

Christian stopped Tex in front of the barn and dismounted. Then he reached up and helped me down.

"Thanks," I said again.

"No problem," he said as he tied Tex to a post near the door. Then we went inside.

"I'm gonna get one of my horses," I said as I pulled a key out of my pocket. I unlocked the tack room. We always kept it locked up when the ranch was open to prevent people from stealing our saddles. I opened the door and went inside. The room was small with little light. Tack was hanging all over the walls. I grabbed a dark bridle off a hook and left the room, locking it behind me.

We started walking down the passage of the barn when I saw something. The Johnsons were standing near one of the stalls.

"What?" Christian asked when he saw me staring at them.

"I hate those people," I answered. "They abuse their horses."

"You wanna go see what they're doin'?" He asked.

"Yeah," I said. We walked closer. I couldn't believe my eyes.

Bryson leaned against the iron bars of the stall door, smiling from ear to ear. Wayde just stood there, looking at the floor, shaking his head.

"Are they selling that horse?" Christian asked.

"They better not," I said.

"Why?"

"It's my horse," I answered, clenching the bridle tightly in my hands. "Go outside and mount Tex. Wait for me."

"Why?" he asked.

"Do you have to know why for everything? Just do it!" I commanded in a loud whisper.

"Get out there soon," he whispered and left the barn.

"Jennifer, what are you doing here?" Grandpa asked, suddenly realizing I was there.

"I'd ask the same thing, but I already know the answer. You said he's my horse!" I snapped.

"You're hurt, and it's the horse's fault. I don't want you to get hurt again," Grandpa explained.

"I get hurt on other horses all the time and you don't sell them," I protested.

"They're not dangerous," Shayne put in as he walked over to where I stood.

"Don't you even start with the dangerous animal crap! Thundering Glory is not dangerous. He just wasn't trained for steer wrestling. It wasn't his fault!" I argued.

"Watch your mouth," Shayne warned.

"I could come up with something worse if you'd like," I shot back.

Wayde cut Shayne off. He walked closer to me and whispered in my ear, "Jennifer, you know that he's a mean horse. We tried to tame him, but it won't work. He won't let anyone ride him, he just throws everyone. Let it go. We'll get you a different horse. Okay?

The tears were coming, but I pushed them back and nodded. "Let me lead him out to the trailer for you, Mr. Johnson," I offered.

"Well, that's more like it," Mr. Johnson smiled.

I went into the stall with Thundering Glory. "You wanna run, buddy?" I whispered in his ear. I slipped the bit into his mouth.

"What are you doing?" Mr. Johnson demanded.

"He'll load the trailer a lot better if he has a bit in his mouth," I explained as I fastened the throatlatch. Then I led him out of the stall. I led him the rest of the way out of the barn. Skyler walked with me.

"We'll be out there in a second," Grandpa said as Mr. Johnson pulled a checkbook out of his pocket.

"What are you doin'?" Christian asked, holding Tex's reins.

"They're making her sell her horse," Skyler said. "Listen, Jennifer, if it was up to me we wouldn't buy your horse."

"You ain't buyin' him anyway. Not over my dead body," I said.

"What are you gonna do?" Christian asked.

"I don't know what to do," I answered.

"Run away," Skyler suddenly said.

"Huh?" I asked.

"You can ride bareback. I've seen you. Get out of here. You've got time. Just go!" Skyler said. "Go with her," he instructed Christian.

"You can't do that!" Christian protested.

"I have to. Don't you see? It's the only link to my father. This horse is all I've got left," I said.

"Do you have any money or anything?" Skyler asked.

"Yeah."

"Are you coming?" I asked Christian.

He didn't answer; he just looked around nervously.

"Look, don't worry," I assured him. "I'm just proving a point. We'll be back before the rodeo next weekend."

"You're sure?" He asked.

"Positive. Skyler, help me up," I said.

He cupped his hands and took my left foot. As he hoisted me onto my horse's bareback, Mr. Johnson yelled from the doorway, "Skyler! What in tarnation do you think you're doin' boy?"

I pulled myself into a sitting position.

"Jennifer! Get off that horse this instant!" Shayne yelled.

I slammed my heels into Thundering Glory's sides and we galloped past everyone, down the drive towards the woods. I heard the pounding of hooves behind me. I looked over my shoulder and saw Christian on Tex, following me. I held Thundering Glory's mane to help me keep my balance. When we got a little way into the woods, I stopped.

"Ya know, maybe this ain't such a good idea," Christian said. "I mean, my Dad's gonna murder me if he finds out."

"Fine! Go on! Go home! I don't want you here with me anyway," I snapped and turned Thundering Glory towards the woods.

"C'mon let's go back," Christian pleaded.

"No! I'm not going back. You can if you want, like I said, I don't care. Nobody's gonna touch this horse ever, ever again. If I have to run away to prove that I'm serious, then so be it!" I trotted further into the woods. I was sure he'd follow me and help me prove my point. I knew he wouldn't leave me alone in the woods. I was wrong. He turned Tex the opposite way and went back to the ranch.

"Fine then," I mumbled to myself. "I don't need you anyway. I'm not going back." I kicked Thundering Glory and cantered farther into the woods.

I rode around for about three hours until I found a small clearing and decided to stay there. It was next to the bottom of a cliff and a stream was nearby. It was one of the places Danny and I had camped a couple of years before with Dad. I dismounted and tied

Thundering Glory to a tree near the stream. He immediately took a long drink and I knelt on the bank and took a drink of the clear water also. "Now what?" I asked Thundering Glory. I couldn't knock the feeling that I was being watched. Then I reminded myself that no one had been out to this part of the woods for a long time, unless Shayne had come out for hunting. Shayne was real big on hunting. Especially deer hunting.

I slipped my boots and socks off and rolled up my jeans. I waded out into the water. It was freezing cold, so I didn't stay in for very long. I climbed back up onto the sandy bank and sat down under Thundering Glory's tree.

"Jennifer," Came a voice from behind me.

I gasped and jumped up. "What are you doing here?" I demanded.

"I came looking for you," Danny answered. "What in the world were you thinking?"

"Go away, Danny," I said and sat back down, leaning my back against the tree.

"Nope. Not until I get an answer," he said and sat down near me. "So you're staying here?"

"Until everyone realizes I mean business. I refuse to sell my horse, especially to the Johnsons. Danny, I can't let them sell him," I said.

Danny looked away and sighed.

"Well, would you sell Double J to them?"

"No, he means too much to me," Danny answered.

"Would Shawn sell Eclipse?"

"No, she's his favorite."

"Would Patrick sell Degenerate?"

"No."

"Do you see what I'm gettin' at?"

Danny paused, then nodded his head. "Totally."

"Thundering Glory means as much to me as Double J means to you," I said. "I can't sell him."

"Do you want me to bring you some stuff later? Maybe something to eat?" Danny offered.

"Would you?" I asked.

"Sure. Anything for Baby Sis," he smiled. I jokingly hit him as he stood up. "I'll be back later," He said as he mounted.

"Bye," I said. I was almost sad to see him go.

He waved as he cantered away.

I laid back against the tree. I was grateful Danny had come looking for me. I hoped he wouldn't tell anyone where I was. I hadn't even thought about food or something to sleep on. I looked at my watch. It was 7:30. I closed my eyes and tried to rest until Danny returned.

Chapter 16

Going Home

Danny came back around 9:30 and by that time I was starving. He brought me a sandwich, an apple, a small bag of chips, a couple of cookies and a canteen of water. He also brought a small tent for me to sleep in.

"You act like you're hungry or something," Danny laughed as he set up the tent.

"I'm starving," I said between bites.

Danny laughed again. Then he turned serious. "Jenn, I wish you would come home. Everyone's worried about you. Olive's about worried herself sick. So have Wayde, Grandpa and Grandma. Blake's real upset and Patrick keeps blaming Bryson and making him feel horrible, like it was his fault."

"It was Bryson's fault," I said hastily, biting into the apple.

"But, Jenny-"

"No. Not until I've proven my point."

"Fine then," Danny said. "Argh! Stupid poles!" he yelled, throwing them on the ground. He walked over to his horse. He came back holding a twenty-two rifle. "Here. I had to borrow this from Shayne. Don't use it unless something like an opossum comes near. All right?"

"Oh, this will do a lot of damage," I said sarcastically.

"It really could. You know to never shoot at someone, even if they-"

"Danny!" I cut him off. "How could you think something like that? I may be bull-headed, but I wouldn't shoot someone!"

"I'm sorry, Jenny," he apologized. "I shouldn't have even thought that. You know how to handle a gun. I'm sorry, I just... I don't know. I'm just so tired, my brain ain't even functioning right now."

"Obviously."

He chuckled and hit my arm. Then he went to finish setting up the tent as I ate the rest of my dinner. "There ya go. I'd better go back before everyone misses me."

"Trust me, Dan, no one will miss you," I said.

"Shut up," he said as he mounted Double J. "I'll be back tomorrow."

I leaned back against a tree and relaxed. Danny had made a small fire and its warmth felt good. It was getting cooler at night. I was lucky Danny had brought me the tent, sleeping bag and a pillow. I crawled into the tent and laid down. I could see the glow of the fire through the tent and I listened to it as it hissed and popped. I started thinking about my dad and how much I missed him. He would have probably been upset that I ran away, but he would have also been proud that I was standing up for something that I believed in. I wondered if Mom would have done the same thing when she was my age, if she had been put in the same situation. She probably would have. Everyone said that I not only looked like her, I acted like her. I wondered if that was why Shayne didn't like me. Maybe I reminded him too much of Mom. I wished I could have talked to her. I wanted to go home, but then they wouldn't take me seriously and they'd sell Thundering Glory. The one thing of my father's that I was trying to hold on to, they were trying to take away. I couldn't let them hurt Thundering Glory, but I knew I couldn't live in the woods in a tent for the rest of my life either. I was trying to decide what to do when I fell asleep.

I spent that whole week in the woods, and it seemed like the longest week in my life. Danny came every day to give me something to eat and he told me what was going on at home.

One afternoon, Danny came to see me, but he wasn't alone.

"Hey, Jenn," Danny said as he rode up.

"Hi," I greeted him. Before I knew what was happening, someone jumped off the back of Danny's horse, ran over to me and choked the life out of me in a hug.

"Where have you been?" the person demanded.

"I can't breathe," I choked out.

"Oh, sorry," he said and let go.

"Blake?" I shrieked.

"Who'd you expect? The Easter Bunny? Or Santa Claus maybe?" he laughed.

I jumped up, furious at Danny. "How could you?" I demanded.

"What?" he asked innocently as he dismounted.

"You promised you wouldn't tell where I was!" I shouted.

"He didn't tell me," Blake said, standing up and brushing the dirt off his jeans. "He showed me. There is a difference."

"Daniel Powell Blackwell, how could you?" I turned away from them, angry tears forming in my eyes.

That was when Blake turned serious. "Jennifer, you can't stay out here forever. Everyone's worried about you and they've been looking for you all week."

"They haven't been looking hard enough," I said.

"They don't have time for crap like this. You need to come home," Blake insisted.

"Nobody cares that I'm gone. Heck, I'll bet some of them are glad to see me go," I said.

"How could you say that?" Danny asked, "We love ya, Jenn. You're everyone's favorite sister!"

"I'm your only sister, you doink," I said.

"Well, it makes you special," Danny said.

"If I'm so special, and everyone loves me so much, then why are they always trying to get rid of Thundering Glory?" I asked.

"They just don't want to see you get hurt, Jenny," Danny said.

"Bryson sure doesn't care," I said.

I think that made Blake mad because then he said, "Now you just wait one minute. You can't judge Bryson. He just doesn't like horses. Just because he's different than you doesn't mean he's a bad person. So, okay, yeah I'll admit it, he's not the easiest person in the world to get along with, but that doesn't matter. Jenn, he's your brother just the way Danny and I are. He loves you too. It's not that he's trying to make your life miserable, he just doesn't want to see you get hurt the way Dad did."

"Thundering Glory would never make a move to hurt me, Blake. He's as gentle as a kitten," I said.

"I wouldn't go that far," Danny said.

Blake ignored him. "You know that, and I know how much that horse loves you, but Bryson can't understand that."

I turned around to face them. "Why? Even when Dad was alive he hated horses. It's not because a horse killed Dad. I think there's something else."

Blake sighed. "Jenn, when Bryson was younger, you don't remember this and neither does Danny, but when Bryson was younger, he loved to ride. He used to jump and everything. He always said he wanted to ride like Dad. But one time, his horse got spooked and Bryson was thrown. He hit his head real bad and was in the hospital, unconscious, for two weeks. He almost died."

"Is that why he's always had trouble in school?" Danny asked.

Blake nodded. "When you got hurt in the rodeo and were sent to the hospital, Bryson was so worried. He was convinced that something had happened to you... because of your horse."

"He was?" I asked.

"Yeah, he was. He has been worried sick about you ever since you took off that day. He hasn't eaten hardly anything and keeps saying it was his fault," Blake answered.

"Jenn, please come home. Nobody's gonna be mad at you. They're just going to be happy that you're okay," Danny begged.

I turned away from them. I couldn't think of anything to say and I didn't know what to do. I knew that if I went home, everyone would be glad to see me, but I wasn't sure if they'd let me keep Thundering

Glory. But if I didn't go home, they'd all worry themselves sick about me, and I didn't want that either. Not even for Bryson or Shayne.

"Well, we'll just be going," Blake said as he and Danny mounted Danny's horse.

"Wait," I said.

"Hmm?" Danny asked.

"I can't take the tent down by myself," I said.

Danny and Blake smiled at each other.

"Don't stand there grinnin' like cats in a bird house, help me pick this stuff up," I commanded. They jumped off the horse and we picked everything up as fast as we could.

We rode home slowly. I didn't say very much, I think I was nervous about facing my family. What Blake had said about Bryson had really surprised me. His story kept rolling around in my head. Had Bryson really liked horses? I couldn't picture him on one in my mind.

We reached the barn and I dismounted, still feeling a bit uneasy about what my family's reaction was going to be. Danny and Blake slid off Danny's horse and we went into the barn. I put Thundering Glory in his stall. He seemed happy to be back and went straight to his feed trough and began munching on the feed that had been left there. Danny put his horse away, too.

"Jennifer?" a familiar voice asked from behind me. I turned around and saw Patrick. He ran over to me and hugged me. "I thought you had been hurt or something. Don't you ever, ever do something like this again! Okay?"

"Okay. I'm sorry. I just didn't want anyone to hurt Thundering Glory. I didn't mean to scare everyone. I'm sorry," I confessed, still hugging my brother.

"Where was she?" Patrick asked.

"Out in the woods. I thought I saw her yesterday, so Blake and I went out to check and there she was," Danny answered.

"You liar," Blake accused.

"Excuse me?" Danny asked.

"You've known where she was since she ran away. I know because I followed you the second day that you went out there. I just kept my mouth shut about it," Blake said.

"You knew the whole time?" I asked.

Blake nodded.

"And you didn't say anything?" I asked again.

"I just figured you'd come home when you felt like it. After I knew you were okay, I just decided to wait and see when you'd come home on your own. But apparently you were just waiting for someone to drag you home by your long, red hair," he smiled.

"You let everyone worry themselves sick while both of you knew the whole time where she was?" Patrick asked.

Blake nodded.

"I oughta kill the both of you," Patrick said, shaking his head.

Blake and Danny laughed.

Ornery ol' Blake. I should have known he'd do something like that. I was mad at first, but then I smiled. I was home.

Chapter 17

Shayne Switches Sides

Of course everyone was shocked when it was suppertime and I casually walked in and sat down at the table. Olive and Grandma cried and everyone hugged me. Grandpa said how happy he was that I was all right and even Shayne said he was happy to see me. Wayde just sat there and smiled at me. After things had calmed down a little bit, he whispered, "I knew you'd come home sooner or later."

Of course, Bryson just sat there frowning at me. Everyone was wondering where I had been and kept asking things like, "Wasn't it cold at night?" or "What about snakes?" Wayde just sat and laughed through most of dinner.

After dinner I volunteered to clear the table, in a way, for worrying everyone. Bryson washed the dishes and Shawn dried them.

"I can't wait for two weeks. It seems like an eternity," Shawn said.

"What are you talkin' about?" Bryson asked, scrubbing a plate with a scratch pad.

"The horse show!" Shawn exclaimed. "Guess what, Jenn?"

"What?" I asked.

"They're having a jumping competition this year! Isn't that great?"

"Oh goody," Bryson mumbled as he rinsed a glass.

"You should show in it," Shawn went on.

Shayne came into the kitchen and stood in the doorway.

"In case you've forgotten, I don't do English riding," I said, another stack of plates to Bryson.

"But I've been thinking and-"

"Don't. You're not used to it," Bryson said dryly. Shayne laughed.

Shawn cleared his throat. "Anyway, I was thinking that, maybe... oh nevermind."

"What?" I asked.

"Nothing. It was dumb. Forget I even said anything."

"Good. Maybe now you'll quit running your jaw," Bryson said.

"Tell me!" I begged.

"Well, I was thinking that maybe you could show Thundering Glory," Shawn said slowly.

Bryson dropped the glass he was washing and it shattered. "Oh, no, you don't. Don't go putting more crazy ideas in her head! Don't you dare!"

"Shawn," I said, "I can't ride Thundering Glory in a show. Who knows what he'd do? He might spook or something. I'm not going to show him."

"See there?" Bryson smiled. "She finally got some sense knocked into her. Maybe she is my sister after all." I shook my head. Bryson continued, "Now we can get rid of that horse. It isn't good for anything. There's no way you could train it to jump in two weeks anyway. Shawn, that was a really stupid idea."

My jaw dropped. I couldn't believe what Bryson had just said. I took a deep breath and looked at Shawn. "Come to think of it, that's a great idea."

"What?" Bryson asked in shock.

"Yes!" Shawn cried.

"Oh, no! Don't even think about it! There is no way you're going to ride that horse anymore anywhere! I don't care if I have to-" Bryson started.

"Bryson!" Shayne cut him off. "Shut up! Nobody wants to hear it!"

Dead silence. Bryson stared at Shayne in disbelief. Shayne had never taken my side on anything before. He was always on Bryson's side.

"What?" Bryson asked.

"You heard me. Shut up," Shayne said slowly. "I don't even want to hear it. That is Jennifer's horse and she can do with it whatever she wants. If she wants to commit suicide on that horse, then so be it. I'm in charge now and I say you'd better just lay off, man. Just..lay..off." With that being said, Shayne turned and left the room. Bryson glared at me for a second, then stormed out the door to the back porch, slamming the screen door behind him. Blake came in just as Shayne got done yelling at Bryson.

Shawn looked at me, smiling, then shrugged. "Oh well," He said and went back to drying and putting away dishes.

"What was that all about?" Blake asked.

"Shayne just told Bryson off," I said.

"For what?"

"He was being a jerk and saying that I couldn't train Thundering Glory to jump. Of course, I'm just going to do it to prove him wrong. Bryson is such a jerk sometimes, isn't he?"

"Yeah," Blake mumbled as he turned around and left.

"What's his problem?" I asked.

Shawn shrugged. "Who knows. Maybe he's just tired."

"Yeah, I guess so," I said and bent down to pick up the pieces of the shattered glass. Shawn started talking about the horse show and what needed to be done to get ready, but I wasn't listening. I was too busy trying to figure out what had just happened.

The next day was Friday. I had forgotten that school started on Monday. It seemed hard to believe that summer was already over. Our school always started before the other school in the district, which made Sarah and I mad, but we couldn't do anything about it.

Sarah and I decided to go shopping for supplies at practically the only store in town that had school supplies: Wal-Mart. Blake drove Sarah, Danny and I to Wal-Mart, then decided to go in himself. We asked him to take us to Columbia, because they had better stores, but he wouldn't.

"I don't want to go back to school," Sarah complained as we walked down the aisle of school supplies.

I shrugged. "I know. Half the things they teach us we'll never even use."

"Like I really care what the capital of Luxembourg is," Danny mumbled.

Sarah and I looked at each other. "What is the capital of Luxem-whatever?" Sarah asked.

"It's Luxembourg. Stupid, huh?" Danny answered.

"Yeah," I mumbled, throwing a notebook in the basket.

"Oh well," Danny shrugged.

We were just finishing our shopping when Blake came over to us. "Ya'll wanna go get some burgers or something?" he asked.

After we left the store, Blake took us to McDonalds. We sat in the play area and got into a food fight. We only stopped when the manager threatened to throw us out. Then we climbed around in the tubes with a couple of little kids. One little kid kept throwing plastic balls at Blake until Blake let her sit on his shoulders. Then, of course, they all wanted a turn. After about half an hour, Blake got tired and said it was time to go home. In the truck the madness continued when Danny pulled a handful of paper covered straws from his pocket and we all started blowing wrappers at each other.

When we got home, we watched a movie with the rest of my brothers.

"I'm gonna have nightmares," Sarah said as Shayne put the cassette in the VCR.

"Child's Play isn't scary," Jeremy argued.

"Is too!" I cut in. "The doll is evil."

"No! Really?" Jeremy asked in fake awe. "I thought he was from the cast of Barney."

"Shut up!" I yelled.

"You'd know who was in Barney, wouldn't you, Jeremy?" Shayne laughed.

"Aw, man, hush. The movie's on," Jeremy mumbled, laughing.

We all settled back to watch the movie. As it got more intense, Sarah drew her knees up to her chin. "Oh my gosh, oh my gosh, oh my gosh. He's gonna kill her. I can't watch!" Sarah exclaimed, covering her eyes with her hands.

"Boo!" Patrick yelled and grabbed Sarah's shoulder. She screamed.

"You jerk! Don't do that!" she yelled, grabbing a handful of popcorn and throwing it at him.

"Patrick, you're a brat," I mumbled and turned back to watch the movie.

"Shut up, Jennifer," he said in a high-pitched, mimicking voice.

"Make me, Patrick," I said.

"Both of ya, knock it off," Shayne scolded.

We sat through the rest of the movie in silence. Danny sat behind Sarah and carefully placed bits of paper in her hair. She didn't realize it until the movie was almost over. She got up and went to the bathroom. She came back and wordlessly punched Patrick.

"What the heck was that for?" Patrick demanded.

"For puttin' paper in my hair!"

"Sarah," I interrupted, "it was Danny."

"Huh?" she looked at me.

"Danny put the paper in your hair," I giggled.

"Danny!" she turned on him and punched his arm. Then she came back over to sit by me.

"I think I deserve an apology," Patrick said.

"I'm so sorry, Patrick," Sarah smiled.

"No, you're not," Patrick fake-sobbed and covered his face.

"Yes I am. I'm sorry," Sarah said and stuck out her bottom lip. "Forgive me?"

"I reckon," Patrick said, imitating Wayde's southern accent.

Sarah laughed.

"I'm tired," Shawn yawned and stretched.

"Me too," Jeremy agreed.

"I'm goin' to bed," I said, getting up. "C'mon, Blondie. You can flirt with my brothers in the morning." I offered her a hand to get up.

"I'm not flirting," she argued, taking my hand and standing up.

"Yes, you are," I said. "Don't worry. He'll still be here in the morning. I promise."

Sarah giggled as we went towards our rooms. Patrick watched us as we climbed the stairs and smiled when Sarah looked back at him. When we go to my room, Sarah flopped down on my beanbag and I laid down on my bed.

"You like Patrick, don't you?" I asked.

"Did it take you that long to figure it out?" she asked.

"What about Josh?" I asked, picking up a "Teen" magazine.

"We broke up," she yawned.

"What?" I asked, sitting up and dropping my magazine. "You broke up with him? When did this happen?"

"About five minutes ago. He just doesn't know it yet," she laughed.

"You would," I said, shaking my head.

"I just did," she snickered. We looked at each other, then burst out laughing. "Patrick is so hot," Sarah sighed.

"I wouldn't know," I told her.

"Well, duh! He's your brother. I'd hope not!" She giggled. Then she turned serious. "You've got to hook me up with Patrick."

"Sarah-" I started.

"Please? C'mon, Jenny," she begged. "I'll hook you up with someone if you get me and Patrick together."

"Oh really? Who?"

"I'll find you someone."

"Oh, I guess I can try," I said.

"Ah! Love you!" Sarah said and got up. "Nighty-night!" Sarah turned the light off and left the room.

Chapter 18

Jennifer Makes a Bet

The next morning Sarah had to leave early, so Shawn and I went out to the barn to start training Thundering Glory to jump. I hated using an English saddle, but it is not allowed to use western saddles in jumping competitions. I led Thundering Glory over to the arena where Shawn had set up cavaletti. Cavaletti are poles lying on the ground that the horse has to go over. There were also a few other jumps set up.

"This should be easy," I said as I mounted up.

"Don't let your head swell. Let Thundering Glory get used to this slowly. Don't just rush in there and-"

"Shawn, my horse. I know. I've been told before. Let me do it. Okay?"

"All right," he sighed and shrugged his shoulders.

We went over the cavaletti like it was nothing. Then we decided to try some of the jumps. They were low and easy to get over. I slowly let Thundering Glory walk up to them and see what they were. But every time I tried to get Thundering Glory to jump, he shied. I almost went over his head one time.

"Try sitting in a forward seat. That might help," Shawn suggested. "He's smart. He'll figure it out soon enough."

I approached the same jump, leaning forward, just as Shawn had said. To my surprise, Thundering Glory jumped. It was a rough little jump, but he jumped it.

Shawn clapped for me. "Do it again!"

I went back around and went over the jump again.

Shawn and I worked the rest of the day with Thundering Glory and even more on Sunday after church.

Sunday evening, Sarah called, talking a million miles an hour about school and how excited she was. I had completely forgotten that the next day we had to go back to school. I became excited also and Sarah and I talked for three hours. We talked until Shayne threatened to disconnect my phone line.

I was so psyched that I had trouble going to sleep that night. But I eventually calmed down and drifted off to sleep.

"Jennifer, wake up," Danny said, shaking my arm.

I sat up sleepily. "Do I gotta?"

"Yeah, c'mon. We hafta get our chores done before we even get ready to go," Danny said as he left the room.

I groaned and slowly got out of bed. I pulled on some old jeans, my boots and an old T-shirt, and then I went outside. I had to water the horses and feed them. Then I ran back inside, determined to get the first shower. Danny came in the other door at the exact same time as I did. We looked at each other, and then we both raced to the top of the stairs and down the hallway. I ran in the bathroom and slammed the door.

"No fair! I get the bathroom first!" Danny yelled, hammering on the door with his fists.

"No way!" I yelled back.

"C'mon, Jenn. I'm older. I get it first!"

"I can't help it that you're slow," I said loudly and turned on the shower.

"Jennifer Elizabeth! C'mon!"

"No!" I laughed.

"Brat!" He slammed his fists on the door one last time to prove his point, then left.

Danny, Patrick and I had to ride the bus because Bryson and Blake didn't want to give us a ride. We walked up to the road at the end of the driveway. Danny put his headphones on and ignored Patrick and me.

"Patrick," I started.

"Hmm?"

"Do you like Sarah?" I asked.

Patrick seemed surprised. "A little. Why?"

"I was just wondering. You're always flirting with her."

"I mean, she's okay. But she's with what's his face. Besides, I'm a little too old for her, ain't I?" Patrick asked, looking through his bag.

"No. She'll turn fifteen in a couple of months. That's not too old. And she broke up with Josh."

"Really? Oh, here comes the bus. Finally!" Patrick sighed and climbed on the school bus.

When I got on I saw two of my friends from junior high, Kelly and Ana.

"Jennifer!" Kelly called. She pointed to a seat directly in front of her. "Sit here."

"Hey. Sup?" I asked, sitting down.

"Not much," Kelly answered, opening her backpack. "Oh shoot! I forgot my trapper-keeper!"

"Arc you nervous?" Ana asked, sitting in front of me.

"Not really. We know a lot of these people up here anyway. It's not like they're all gonna kill us because we're from Renick you guys," I said.

Ana, Kelly, Sarah and I had gone to school together since Kindergarten at a small school. The town was small, two hundred people to be exact. Renick didn't have a high school, so we had to choose where we went to high school. Half of us decided to go to Moberly Senior High School.

"Yeah, because your brothers go out here," Ana said.

"Jeremy said that if anyone messes with me, he's gonna kick their butt," I said. "But, Kelly, you have a sister that goes out here. Don't you know some people?"

"I don't claim Dana anymore," she scoffed. "I can't believe I forgot my trapper."

"You don't need it the first day anyway," Ana said.

"You don't?" Kelly asked. "Whew. Thank goodness. I thought I was gonna be in trouble the first day of school."

I pulled my discman out of my bag and put in my Backstreet Boys Millennium C.D.

When we got to the school, Sarah ran up to us. "Hey, Jenn!"

"Hey," I said, looking around. "I'm already lost."

Sarah laughed. "Me too, and my mother works here! But at least we're out of Renick, right?"

"Speak for yourself," Ana mumbled.

"Really," I mumbled, looking at the map of the school. "Sarah, do I have any classes with you?"

"I don't think so chick," she answered, chewing on her fingernails.

"Well, we'd better find our first hour class," Ana decided and grabbed Kelly's arm and mine and pulled us down a crowded hallway. It took us ten minutes to find our class. And it only took us thirty seconds to realize we had walked past it four times and was right next to the door we came in. First hour was the only class I had with Ana and Kelly, so the rest of the day I was on my own.

Luckily I had the same lunch hour as Ana and Kelly so I sat with them. Unfortunately, Sarah had third lunch, so I didn't get to see her.

"Are we having fun yet?" I jokingly asked as I sat down at the table.

Ana's eyes got big and she shook her head. "No! I hate it here. These hallways are so confusing. I keep getting lost!"

Kelly laughed. "I know. Me too. It took me forever to find my algebra class."

"That's the class I just came from," I said. "I just wanna go home." I looked through my lunch box.

Ana nodded in agreement.

"May I sit here?" a girl asked.

"I guess," I shrugged.

"Aren't you two on the softball team?" the girl asked.

Ana and Kelly nodded.

"I'm Katie. I'm on the team too."

We introduced ourselves to Katie.

"Is it okay if some of my friends sit over here?" she asked.

"Sure," we agreed.

"Megan!" Katie hollered. "Over here!" She motioned to her friend to sit with us.

A girl with shoulder length brown hair walked over and sat beside Kelly. "Hi," she said quietly and smiled. She seemed very shy.

We all started talking about how high school was so different from elementary school and how it was nothing like what we'd expected. Several other people joined us, friends of Megan and Katie. I recognized a couple of the boys from my art class.

"Look at that guy over there," one girl said, pointing. "He is so hot!"

I looked to whom she was pointing at and smiled.

"Who is that? Does anyone know?" she asked, practically drooling all over the table.

Megan shrugged.

"I know who that is," I mumbled.

Ana smiled at me and started to giggle. She'd recognized the boy also.

"Who?" The girl demanded.

"Jeremy Blackwell. He's a senior. He's got a girlfriend though," I said.

"How do you know?" she asked.

"He's my brother," I said.

"How long has he had a girlfriend?"

"About a year and a half now, I reckon," I said.

The girl shrugged and went back to flirting with the boys from my art class.

That was when someone tapped me on the shoulder. I turned around to see a really pretty blonde sophomore standing behind me. Her hair was half way down her back and tied back. She was wearing an Old Navy T-shirt and jean shorts. "You're Jennifer Blackwell, aren't you?"

"Yeah, why?" I asked.

"Scoot over," she told Katie and pushed her out of the way to sit beside me. "You have horses, right?"

"Yes," I said.

"I've heard you have a really pretty horse that you're going to show in a competition next weekend," she went on.

I was getting suspicious. "That's right, although I don't see how it concerns you."

She giggled. "Skyler Johnson was telling me that he has a horse that he's going to enter in the competition."

"Yeah. White Liberty, right?"

"I guess so. Anyway, he also told me that the horse you are going to enter," she stopped to push back a few blonde strands of hair that had fallen over her eyes, "was supposed to be his horse. But, as it turns out, you threw a fit when your grandparents went to sell it, so they let you keep it. Is that right?"

"I didn't throw a fit," I said hastily. "He's my horse and nobody but me can sell him. It was my brothers that were trying to sell him, not Grandpa."

"Ooh, so snippy! Why didn't you sell it to them?" she asked.

"Because they abuse their animals," I said loudly. The cafeteria was growing quiet as more people stopped their conversations to listen to us. "I was not about to sell my horse to someone who was going to beat him."

"They don't beat their horses, they just show them who is in charge," she tried to explain.

"They don't have to show them who is in charge by hitting them. If they'd try a little kindness, I'd bet they'd be surprised!"

"Skyler is kind to the horses," she said, standing up.

That was when it registered. This was Skyler's girlfriend. "Yeah, right," I mumbled.

"I'm glad he didn't buy your stupid horse anyway. Who wants a dangerous animal that goes around killing people?" she asked loudly, walking away.

"He didn't do it on purpose!" I yelled. "Besides, how would you know? You wouldn't know a good horse from a bad one if it bit you on your rich, spoiled butt!"

She spun around and glared at me, her blue eyes flaming. "Would you like to make a little bet? I'll bet you fifty bucks that Skyler's horse beats your horse at the competition next weekend."

"Fine," I said, standing up. "But let's make this interesting. Let's double that bet and the loser also has to muck out the other's stable for a month," I challenged.

"Do it, Judy!" someone yelled.

"Even better," she said and stuck out her hand for me to shake.

I took her hand and gripped it as hard as I could. She winced, but didn't cry out.

"C'mon, Ana," I motioned for Ana and Kelly to follow me as I walked past Judy.

The next thing I heard was Ana's voice saying, "Oops, I'm so sorry." I turned around to see the front of Judy's shirt soaked with Pepsi. Ana had a smiled on her face and an empty soda can in her hand. "That was so clumsy of me," Ana said, sarcastically.

Kelly's eyes were wide and her mouth hung open. She immediately covered her mouth with her hand to keep from laughing. Then she said, “You should really be more careful, Judy.”

Judy's mouth also hung open. "Gross!" she shrieked.

"You think that's gross? You're gonna love cleaning stables for a month!" Patrick called from his table. Then he, Danny, Trevin and Brandon burst out laughing.

"C'mon, guys," I said and together Kelly, Ana and I left the cafeteria.

Chapter 19

The End of the First Day

After school I met up with Sarah, who was waiting outside near the trees that were at the front of the school.

"Hey," she said as I walked up.

"Hi," I mumbled.

"You all right?" she asked.

"Mm-hmm. I'm just tired," I yawned.

Sarah yawned also. "Me too," she laughed.

"Hey, Sarah! Hey, Jennifer!" Danny called, walking toward us with Patrick. "Jennifer, that was so funny at lunch."

"What happened?" Sarah asked.

"Jennifer almost got into a fight with Skyler Johnson's girlfriend," Patrick laughed. "It was so funny..."

Out of the corner of my eye I saw Skyler and some of his friends in the parking lot. Judy was with them, hanging all over Skyler. I didn't know why, but for some reason I was suddenly jealous. Skyler looked back at me. We just stared at each other for a minute, and then I turned away.

"Hey, Shorty, you plannin' on walkin' home?" Blake asked.

"Are you sure you want to be seen with me in your truck?" I asked sarcastically.

"You can duck down in the floor board," Patrick laughed and climbed into the cab.

"You guys are mean!" I yelled.

"Oh, well, I guess she doesn't want a ride. We'll just tell Grandpa you decided to walk home," Blake said, opening the door to the truck. "C'mon, Danny!"

Danny ran over to the truck and threw his books into the back. "C'mon, Jenn." He offered me a hand and helped me into the truck bed.

"Let's go!" I yelled at Blake. "Danny, who are we waitin' on?"

"Jeremy. Here he comes," Danny answered.

Jeremy threw his bag in the back of the truck and hopped in, sitting down across from me. Danny leaned against the back of the cab. Patrick and Bryson sat in the front with Blake, who was driving. Blake revved the engine, peeled out of the student parking lot and flew over the speed bump. He didn't care that he was supposed to slow down. He was too busy showing off for his friends in the parking lot to care. It worried me, his reckless driving I mean, because I was still paranoid about what had happened with Patrick. But it was fun to ride with Blake and he would at least slow down if he knew he could get hurt.

When we got onto the highway, Blake sped up even more. My hair swirled around my face so that I could hardly even see.

"I can't see anything!" I laughed, trying to control my hair.

"You need to cut it," Jeremy said.

"Never! I like it this way," I smiled.

"Only because Mom used to wear it that way," Jeremy mumbled.

"What?" I asked. "Is that bad or something?"

"No, but you just remind everyone of her so much. Maybe too much, ya know?" I'm not trying to be mean, but you do. You look exactly like her. I know you remind Shayne of her," Jeremy said. He studied a bruise on his knee; more than likely caused by playing football with is friends.

We were all suddenly very quiet. "Do you remember her, Jeremy?" I asked.

"A little," he answered, looking up at the sky.

"What do you remember?"

"I dunno," he shrugged.

"Yes, you do. Tell me," I insisted.

“Well . . ." he said, thinking. "I remember how she used to play the piano. The only time I remember hearing her play it was one year at Christmas. She played that song . . . oh, what was it? I can't remember it now." Jeremy snapped his fingers. "Hark the Harold Angels Sing. That was it. Mom loved that song. And Carol of the Bells. It was so pretty . . . I miss her." Jeremy sighed.

Neither Danny nor I said anything. I didn't know what to say. I was suddenly feeling guilty again. We rode the rest of the way home in silence.

Chapter 20

Remembering Mom and Dad

The subject came up again that evening when all my brothers and I were in the barn. Blake was shoveling out stalls and Danny was unsaddling Double J. It surprised me that anyone even said anything, but all of the sudden, out of thin air, Jeremy asked, "Shayne, what do you remember about Mom?"

Shayne seemed shocked by the question. "I don't know," he answered, holding a lunge line whip in his hands. "Why?"

"I dunno. Just what do you remember?" Jeremy asked again.

Shayne leaned back against the stable door and crossed his arms, moving the whip in small, circular motions. "I remember how she used to sing us to sleep when we were little. Remember that, Shawn?"

"Yeah," Shawn answered.

"Dad used to play the guitar and Mom would sing that song, it was a Disney song, what was it?" Shayne asked.

“Baby Mine. It was from Dumbo," Shawn smiled. "I just about wore that tape out, I watched it so often when I was younger. I wonder what happened to it?"

Shayne shrugged, then hc laughed. "I remember at Christmas she always played the piano and we would push the keys and mess up her songs."

"I remember that now too, now that you've said that," Jeremy said, smiling.

"Didn't Dad used to sing?" Blake asked.

"Dad always sings," Danny said, brushing Double J. Then he corrected himself. "I mean, used to sing."

Shayne nodded. "Mom would play the piano and Dad would play the guitar . . ." Shayne's voice trailed off. He bit his bottom lip and looked at the floor.

There was a silence and Bryson asked, "You all right, bro?"

Shayne nodded and kept his head down. His knuckles on his right hand, I noticed, were white from gripping the whip.

"I wish I could remember Mom," Patrick said.

"You were three when she died, don't you remember anything?" Shawn asked.

"I sort'a do. I just remember a really pretty voice," Patrick answered. "And I was only two and a half."

"Well, whatever," Shawn shrugged.

Danny suddenly laughed out loud. "Remember how Dad used to pick us up by our arms and swing us around? And the tree swing? He'd push us on it and we'd jump out."

Shayne sniffed. "I miss them," He said quietly and looked up. His eyes were turning blood shot and he angrily wiped tears away. He quickly looked back at the ground.

"Are you all right?" Patrick asked.

Again, Shayne nodded.

I had been silent the whole time. I was sitting on a hay bale, my knees up to my chest and my chin resting on them. I just sat there, listening to my brothers reminis about my parents. It scared me to see Shayne cry. I couldn't even remember seeing him cry at Dad's funeral, and here he was, crying right in front of everyone.

Shayne suddenly cussed and threw the whip. He punched the stall door, causing Degenerate to whinny, and fell back against it. Shayne folded his arms and sank to the floor. "I can't believe we lost them both."

"It's all right, man. We'll be all right," Blake assured Shayne.

"No, it's not! We lost Mom . . . and now we've lost Dad. It isn't fair. You realize what we are, don't you? We're orphans!" Shayne yelled back.

I hadn't thought of it that way. It was true though and it was my fault.

"There's nothing wrong with that," Jeremy said.

"I don't care. It doesn't have anything to do with it. It's not fair. It's just not fair they left us here!" Shayne slammed his arm against the stall door. "They just left us!" He dropped his head to his knees.

Bryson looked away, leaning against one of the supporting posts. He looked like he was ready to cry also.

Everyone was silent for a long time.

"It's my fault," I said quietly.

"What?" Shayne asked, looking up.

"I said, 'It's my fault!' If I hadn't been born, Momma never would have died and she'd still be here!" I cried loudly. "And if I wasn't so horse crazy, Dad would not have gotten hurt. It's all my fault."

"Hey! Don't you ever, *ever* say that again, do you understand me?" Shayne yelled sternly. "I never want to hear you blame yourself for their deaths! True, there were complications when you were born, but it wasn't your fault. You couldn't help it that you were born.

And thank God you lived through it. You almost died too, ya know? And Dad would have bought that horse whether or not you liked it. It is not you fault."

"Yes, it is," I whispered and looked at the floor.

"No, it's not," Shayne insisted. "Why would you think that?"

"You've always blamed me for Mom's death," I shot back. "Why shouldn't I believe it?"

"What?" Shayne cried.

"Jenn, we've never blamed you for Mom's death," Jeremy said slowly, a look of pure shock on his face. "None of us."

"But it's my fault!" I wailed. I tried my hardest, but I couldn't stop. I burst into tears. "It's all my fault." I dropped my head onto my knees and cried.

"Shh," One of my brothers, I thought it was Blake, but I couldn't tell, whispered and put his arm around my shoulders. "It's not your fault."

I leaned into his shoulder and cried harder. "Yes, it is."

"Why do you think that?" he asked, still whispering.

"Blake, you know why. Bryson and Shayne both blame me for it and you know that's true. Bryson hates me . . . and he has every right. It's my fault," I sobbed.

"I don't hate you!" he said and pushed me away. "Jenny, I love you, you're my sister!"

I looked up. "Wha - Bryson?" It hadn't been Blake that put his arm around me, it was Bryson. I didn't know what to do. I wanted to get up and run, but my knees wouldn't work. I just sat there and stared at him.

"Jennifer, I could never hate you. Why would you think that?" Bryson asked.

“I . . . well, I mean . . . it's just . . . you just act like you can't stand me," I stammered.

Without another word, Bryson pulled me close and hugged me, practically squeezing the life out of me." I could never hate you, Jenn. I'm sorry," he whispered.

"You mean that?" I asked.

"Yeah, Jenn. I don't hate you. I just worry about you getting hurt. We've lost Mom, we've lost Dad, can't afford to lose you too."

"Yeah, Jenny. You're the only sister we got," Blake said. "I mean, if we lose a brother, we still have five more, but we lose you and that's it. You're the only one we got."

"The only one we have," Shawn corrected him.

"That's what I just said," Blake laughed.

I had quit crying by then. I wished I had some of my own memories about my mother. I wished my Dad was still there. I kept thinking about it and felt like crying again. Then I thought about the family I still had left and I realized how blessed I really was. I was lucky to still have my brothers and grandparents. They would take care of me.

"Can you tell me more about what you remember about Mom?" I asked Shayne.

He sighed heavily. "Where do you want me to start?"

"Anywhere," I answered.

Chapter 21

The Boys Ride Thundering Glory

The next day at school I was really tired. I hadn't gotten very much sleep because I had stayed in the barn with my brothers until midnight and then I stayed up even later to watch TV. It almost killed me to get up at four thirty to take care of the horses and I slept the whole bus route. I was exhausted and I kept falling asleep in all my classes, which isn't the best thing to do the second day of school. I talked to a lot of people when I wasn't sleeping, which didn't go over too well with the teachers either. I was really getting off to a bad start, with the teachers that is. I was making a lot of friends, but we kept getting in trouble because we couldn't quit talking. I also got lost going from the choir room to the geography room until I followed someone that I recognized from the day before. I met up with Sarah and Ana after school.

"Where's Kelly?" I asked.

"She went home with her sister," Ana replied. "Where's your brothers?"

"I dunno," I said.

"I wanna go over to your house," Sarah whined. "It's boring at my house."

"I gotta work with Thundering Glory for the jumping competition. It's this weekend and I'm not sure if he's ready. I made a big bet and I hafta win this or I'm in big trouble," I told her.

"Jumping? Isn't that English style riding?" Sarah asked.

"Unfortunately," I answered.

Ana made a face. "Unfortunately? I like to ride English. I don't ride very often, but I like it when I do."

"Good for you," I said.

"I am going home with you," Sarah said very matter-of-factly. "I'll just talk to someone while you ride."

"That someone wouldn't be Patrick, would it?" I teased.

"What?" Ana asked. "Patrick? Sarah you like Patrick?"

"Maybe," Sarah shrugged and giggled.

"Did you break up with Josh?" I asked.

"Uh-huh. I just told him that we hardly ever get to see each other anymore now that I'm in high school and he's still in Junior high. So now I'm free to do whatever I want. I'm a free woman!" Sarah yelled and laughed.

I rolled my eyes. "I guess you can come over."

"Ana's coming too!" Sarah exclaimed.

"I can't," Ana said. "I have to go home. My mom is making me clean my room."

"Bummer," Sarah mumbled. "Oh! There's Blake and Patrick! Let's go, Jenn." Sarah grabbed my arm and pulled me towards the truck. "Hi!"

"Hey, Kit-Kat," Patrick said, smiling.

Sarah smiled back. "Everyone's calling me that now because of softball. I like my new nick-name."

"I guess we gotta take this blonde home with us," I mumbled.

"Ah! How rude!" Sarah slapped my arm. "You're mean to me, Jenny."

"I try," I said smiling.

"Ya'll wanna go drivin' around for awhile?" Blake asked." Shayne's driving."

"Yeah!" Sarah jumped up and down like a little child.

"Hop in," Patrick said.

"Oh, goody!" Sarah exclaimed and climbed into the back of the truck.

"You're an idiot," I said as I followed her into the truck bed.

"Shut up!" Sarah yelled and hit me again.

"A hyper idiot," Patrick said, sitting down next to us. Sarah hit him too.

"Do you get some sort of sick pleasure by causing physical harm to people other than yourself?" Patrick asked.

Sarah thought about it for a minute then cried, "Yes!" and hit him again.

I rolled my eyes and mumbled, "Flirt." Sarah turned to smile at me. I just shook my head.

Blake got into the back of the truck with us and Shayne started the engine.

We drove around until it got dark then we dropped Sarah off at her house. I don't think her parents were too pleased with her not coming home right after school, but they didn't say anything. At least, they didn't say anything to us. I was a little bit concerned, but she just smiled and waved good-bye.

I was also a little bit upset because I didn't get to work with Thundering Glory. I guess Shayne just lost track of time.

The next day I came home right after school to work with Thundering Glory. I brushed and saddled him and Danny got out Double J.

"Why are you puttin' an English saddle on him?" I asked.

"I just thought I felt like jumping today, okay?" Danny asked as he tightened the cinch.

"Does Double J jump?" I asked. I couldn't remember him jumping before.

"We'll find out, won't we?" Danny smiled.

I mounted Thundering Glory. "You're nuts," I mumbled.

Danny smiled and mounted. "Thank you."

"Hey, Danny, I'll race ya to the arena," I challenged.

"Ready . . . set . . . go!" He yelled and kicked Double J.

We galloped our horses as fast as they could go all the way to the arena. We beat Danny and Double J.

Shawn turned to look at us as we entered the building. "Howdy!" he called in his most southern accent.

"Sup?" I nodded.

"Well, give her a go," he said and opened the gate for me. Thundering Glory trotted through it then cantered towards the first jump. We had a pretty good run-through. We weren't near as fast as we should have been, but we went clear, meaning we didn't knock over any rails.

"How was it?" I asked, pulling up next to the gate.

"Well, he was a little low on the third jump and you weren't near fast enough. I've been watching

Skyler Johnson and his horse and they're gonna be hard to beat," Shawn answered.

"You think you can do better?" I asked as Danny trotted over on Double J.

"Let me go get Eclipse," Shawn said and turned to leave the arena.

"No. This horse. Let me see what you can do with him. If you can do better, then I'll listen to you."

"All right, get off," he said.

I dismounted and handed the reins to Shawn.

"Are you crazy?" Danny asked, reaching down to grab Shawn's arm. "That horse will murder you!"

At the same time, Blake walked into the arena. "Wassup?" he called.

"Shawn thinks he can ride Thundering Glory," Danny answered.

"Hey, can I ride him?" Blake asked.

"Oh, by all means, please do," Shawn said hastily. He really gets a big head when it comes to jumping. He thinks he's the only one in the family who knows anything about it.

Blake strolled through the gate and walked over to Shawn. Shawn practically threw the reins at Blake. "Thanks, buddy," Blake said.

"Be careful," I warned.

"I know," Blake mumbled and walked to Thundering Glory's near side. He stood near Thundering Glory's shoulder, stroking his neck and speaking quietly to him. Then Blake put his foot in the stirrup and quickly pulled himself up. Thundering Glory stood still with his head up and his ears going backwards and forwards, listening to Blake as he said quietly, "Easy, boy, easy." Then Blake clucked to him and urged him to canter. Blake's fearlessness must have taken over him because he ran the course like it was nothing. He didn't go very fast, but he was used to bronco riding, so jumping came easy for him.

Blake slowed Thundering Glory down and nervously said, "See? No sweat." He dismounted and I think we were all in shock, including Blake. He led Thundering Glory over to us and handed me the reins. Blake's hands were shaking, but I didn't say anything.

"All right, my turn," Shawn said and took the reins.

"You gonna be all right?" Danny asked.

"I hope," Shawn murmured. He nervously mounted and ran the course slowly. On the second time around, he sped up a lot. Thundering Glory flew over the jumps. I don't think I've ever seen a horse take the jumps so quickly in all my life.

Shawn was smiling from ear to ear when he rode up next to us.

"Wow," I said. "I've never seen a horse take the jumps that fast before."

"I have," Blake said.

"Oh yeah. Remember Midnight Skies? He used to do that," Shawn said.

"Who?" I asked.

"Midnight Skies. Oh, you probably don't remember. It was the horse that Bryson - never mind," Shawn stopped himself.

"What?" I asked.

"Remember how we told you that Bryson got hurt when he was younger?" Danny asked.

"Yeah. So?"

"Midnight Skies was the horse," Danny answered.

"Oh, I see," I said. "What happened to the horse?"

"I think they sold it because Bryson hated it so much after that," Shawn said.

"I wish there was a way to get Bryson to ride again," I said wishfully.

"Yeah," Shawn sighed.

After a short silence, Blake started to smile.

"What? Blake, don't grin like that. You're scaring me, man," Danny said.

I knew that smile. Blake was up to something. You could see it in his eyes. Something was turning in his head and we all knew we would have to go along with it, no matter how crazy it was going to be. You just didn't say “no” to Blake. He would get an idea and everyone would just run with it. There was just something that made you want to go along with him on every single little thing he did. And he never, ever got into trouble. He got away with everything.

I smiled, too. "Tell me."

"Don't encourage him!" Shawn exclaimed.

"Tell me," I said again, ignoring Shawn.

"Not now. Later. Let me work this out in my head first," Blake grinned. "I wonder where Patrick is," he mumbled then ran out of the building, yelling, "Patrick! C'mere!"

I shook my head. "I can't wait to see what he comes up with," I said as I mounted Thundering Glory.

"You just had to encourage him, didn't you?" Shawn asked.

"What? It's not like anything I say or do will discourage him," I argued.

"Oh!" Shawn sighed exhasperatedly. "Just get back to practicing. We'll worry about them later."

Chapter 22

Jennifer gets in a Fight

On Friday, I went to school, excited beyond excitement.

"You seem happy today," Ana said when she saw me, right before first hour began.

"I am! I am!" I jumped up and down.

"Why?" she asked, her eyes bright.

"Tomorrow's the jumping competition," I told her.

"Jumping competition?" she asked, puzzled.

"You know. Horses? Jumping? Big deal, large bet. Extremely large bet."

"You shouldn't have bet that girl money," Ana said.

"Yeah, but it's too late now. It's a done deal. And I hope that Thundering Glory wins. Otherwise, it'll be 'hello Johnson stables' for me," I told her.

Ana laughed at me.

"Not funny," I said. "This is serious. It's taken me awhile to save up a hundred bucks. I was going to use it to help me pay for my next horse. I really need this money, Ana."

Ana shrugged innocently. "Sorry."

"I have to go home right after school and set everything up for the competition," I said.

"That sounds like fun," Ana rolled her eyes.

"It will be."

"Sure," she shrugged.

"Oh, you don't know nothin'," I said.

"Oh, look. It's the girl that wishes she was better than me," Judy's voice said behind me to a couple of her rich, snobby friends. One of them giggled.

"I am better than you," I said, turning to face her, my eyes narrowing.

"You wish," one of her friends said.

"Shut up, you airhead," I snapped.

"You are such a tomboy," Judy said, ignoring her friend, who looked hurt at my insult.

"I'd rather be a tomboy than a prep," I said casually, "Cityslicker." I didn't wait for her to reply and went to sit at my desk. Luckily, the bell rang and class started. I could hear them snickering at me from across the room, but I tried to ignore it. It's hard to ignore something, though, when someone's laughing and you know that you're the joke. It hurts. I felt like crying or hitting a wall or something, but I decided against it. That was what they wanted me to do. The last thing I wanted to do was let them think that they were getting to me. I could wait until after school, or at least until after class.

"Don't let them bug you," Kelly whispered.

"They aren't," I told her.

"She's snobby."

"I could've told you that."

Kelly snickered.

After what seemed like hours, the bell finally rang. Everyone jumped up and headed out the door. Somehow, I ended up next to Judy in the hall.

"Oh, what is that smell?" she asked.

"Probably your boyfriend," I said.

"No, I think it's you," She said.

"Shut up." I suddenly threw my weight against her and slammed her into a locker.

"Get off me," she shoved me away.

"You wanna start somethin'?" I yelled.

"Yeah!" she jumped up.

"Well come on!" I held my arms out from my sides. I had seen Patrick do that when he got into a fight with one of his now ex-friends. I can't remember what they were fighting about. I think it was over a girl.

Judy stood up to me. "Don't start nothin' with me," she warned in a low voice.

"Oh, you done started it," I said. "Now I get to finish it."

Judy's eyes burned into mine. I stared right back.

"Don't look at me like that," she commanded and pushed me.

I pushed her back. She stumbled back a few steps, then shoved me again. I threw the first punch.

We got into quite a little fight until Blake and Skyler saw us and pulled us apart. Skyler grabbed Judy's shoulders and pulled her away while Blake had me around my waist. We were still screaming at each other when the principal, Mr. Stephens, walked up.

"What's going on here?" he demanded.

"It's - it's all right now," Blake tried to explain.

"What's the problem?" Mr. Stephens asked.

"She pushed me," Judy said, pointing at me.

"You started it!" I yelled at her.

"Whatever!" She yelled back, Skyler still holding her by her shoulders.

"You did!"

"Did not!"

"Did to!"

"Enough!" Mr. Stephens suddenly yelled, his face turning bright red. "My office, both of you! That's it! Show's over!" He tried to herd everyone back to their classes. Then he led Judy and I to his office.

"Nice going," I whispered.

Judy shot me a look that scared even me.

"Have a seat," Mr. Stephens sat down behind his desk. "Now what's the problem?"

"The problem is she needs to shut her big mouth," Judy said, pointing at me again.

"No, the problem is she has a snotty little attitude and I'm sick of it," I said.

"What is this all about?" Mr. Stephens asked.

"Okay, she comes here, actin' like she's all better than everyone else and thinkin' she's all that because her Grandparents own a bunch of stupid horses. Like everyone should baby her because some stupid horse killed her Dad and she's an orphan or whatever now," Judy said.

I could've jumped up and belted her right then and there. I was really hurt because I was still trying to get used to the idea that Dad was really gone. I almost did hit her, but Mr. Stephens shook his head at me.

"Judy, you shouldn't say things like that. That's very rude. Jennifer, what is your problem with Judy?" he asked, turning to look at me.

"Well, you just heard her. Can't you see how snobby she is? I'm just sick of her attitude. She better adjust it, or I'll adjust it for her," I said, looking right at her. She looked away.

"Girls, do I have to call your parents?" Mr. Stephens seemed to be running out of patience.

Judy shrugged.

"My Grandparents aren't home. Call Shayne. He's home," I suggested, leaning back in the chair.

"Girls, you don't really want me to call your parents and have them come out here, do you?"

"Go for it," I said dully.

"Fine," Mr. Stephens mumbled something to himself, getting up. "You just stay right there." He left the office, leaving Judy and I there by ourselves.

I got up and started to walk around the office. I yawned. "This is stupid. Shayne'll probably either kill me or laugh at me. I hope he laughs."

"My mom's gonna kill me," Judy said.

"It's not that big of a deal. It was just a little fist fight," I said, picking up a picture and looking at it. It was Mr. Stephens and his wife and children.

Judy giggled.

"What?" I asked.

"Your lip. It's busted," she giggled.

I felt around with my tongue until I tasted something salty. "Yuck," I made a face. "Your eye's bruised."

Judy dropped her head in her hands and started to cry.

"What's wrong now?"

"I'm gonna be in so much trouble. Skyler probably won't like me anymore if my face is all bruised."

"Oh, my gosh," I said, stressing each word. "You really are an airhead!"

"Shut up!"

"Who cares about Skyler anyway?" I asked.

"I do," she said.

"You don't deserve him," I mumbled.

"What?" she looked up.

"None of your business," I said, sitting down.

"You know I'm more popular than you," she said suddenly, lowering her voice again. "You know I can ruin your reputation, or at least what's left of it."

"You know I'm more intelligent, I'm prettier, and I've got the more appealing personality," I said, lowering my own voice. "You know I can ruin your face, or at least what's left of it."

I had just finished my sentence when Mr. Stephens opened the door to the office. "Your families are on the way," he said. "I have to go to the cafeteria, something about the oven catching on fire. You stay here and behave." Then he left.

I busted up laughing. Judy looked away to avoid laughing.

We sat and waited for our families to come. Judy's mother burst through the door and rushed to her daughter. "Oh Judy, darling, are you all right?"

"I'm okay, Mom. I'm okay," she said.

"Judith," A stern voice said from the doorway.

"Dad!" Judy seemed alarmed. "You're home?"

"Mm-Hmm," he nodded. He was tall and dark, and looked very upset with Judy.

Judy's mother looked at me. "Is this the girl who got you into trouble?"

Judy nodded.

"Ah, Mr. and Mrs. Smith," Mr. Stephens said, coming into the office and closing the door behind him. "I'm pleased that you could take time out of your day and come down here."

"What's the problem?" Mr. Smith asked.

"Well, your daughter and this young lady seem to have a little misunderstanding," Mr. Stephens started to explain.

The door burst open again and this time Shayne stormed through it. "Which one did it this time?"

Mr. Stephens pointed at me.

Shayne turned. The look on his face was pure shock at first, then it changed. I expected to see anger, sadness or for the shock to stay. But none of those was what I got. The look Shayne gave me was none other than approval. Now it was my turn to be shocked. Shayne walked over and stood behind me.

Mr. Stephens sat up straighter and cleared his throat. "Now that everyone's here, maybe we can work something out."

"What happened?" Shayne asked.

"Your daughter practically attacked our Judy," Mrs. Smith said.

"First off, this is my sister. Our Dad wasn't available to come down here. So I came instead," Shayne answered.

"Anyhow, she hit my daughter. I know Judy had nothing to do with this, or at least she didn't fight. Judy would never do something like that," Mrs. Smith said.

"Well, Mrs. Smith, actually I think that both girls had a part in this," Mr. Stephens said.

Mrs. Smith was appalled. "Never," she gasped.

"Oh I suppose I punched myself in the mouth then, didn't I?" I said.

Shayne snickered behind my back.

"Jennifer, keep the comments to yourself," Mr. Stephens warned.

"No," I said. "I am tired of people telling me what to do. She is just as guilty as I am. I admit it, I started it. But she was in on it too!"

"Jennifer, that will be enough," Mr. Stephens said.

"You see? She admits she started it!" Mrs. Smith said.

"Donna, you're too upset. Maybe you should step outside," Mr. Smith suggested.

"What? But-"

"Go on," he ushered her out the door. "Now, I think we can continue."

"Well, I think that we should decide on what is to be done about this whole thing," Mr. Stephens said.

"I can assure you, Judy will be punished when she gets home."

"Daddy!" Judy protested.

"You will do chores without complaining, do you understand me?" he asked.

She nodded and looked at me again.

Mr. Stephens nodded. "I think that's suitable for the home punishment, Mr. Smith."

"What?" I shrieked. "She-"

Shayne clapped a hand over my mouth. "That's full'a crap. Jennifer has chores every single day, and that's not even a punishment. She gets up, we all get up, before five o'clock in the morning to take care of the horses. That's not even fair!"

"Shayne," Mr. Stephens held up a hand to silence my defensive older brother. "We haven't decided the punishment for school. Mr. Smith was merely stating the home punishment."

Shayne sighed heavily. Shayne never did like authority...

"Now, the punishment for fighting, according to the handbook, is O.S.S. for the appropriate amount of time," Mr. Stephens said. "So I think that both girls will have to miss out on school Monday and Tuesday of next week, since this is only their first offense. If it happens again, the amount of days will be extended. Understood?"

Judy and her father nodded.

I turned around to look at Shayne. His eyes flamed.

Mrs. Smith came back in, stating, "I just can't stay out there in the hallway any longer."

"We're just about done here," Mr. Stephens said. "Girls, I also think that an apology is in order."

"Sorry," Judy mumbled.

I stood up and headed for the door.

"Um, Jennifer. Apology?" Mr. Stephens said.

I turned to look at Judy. Her mother was looking her over, making sure she was all right.

"I'm sorry," I said as sincerely as possible.

"Well, I'm not," Shayne had his hand on my shoulder, pushing me towards the door. Then he spoke both our feelings. "She deserved it. Maybe it'll bring her down to earth, make her realize she's no better than anyone else is. 'Cause she sure ain't any better than my sister. Nobody's better than Jenny. Nobody," then turning to Mr. Stephens, "Understood?" With that, he picked up my fifteen-pound backpack and heaved it into my stomach and shoved me out the door.

"C'mon," he said, heading for the front office.

"Where are we going?" I asked.

"Home. You're not staying here. I'm tired of him," Shayne said.

"I get to leave?" I asked as the bell rang.

Shayne nodded. "I'm gonna get Patrick. He can help set up for the jumping competition. He'd rather do that than sit through Geometry."

"Hi Shayne!" Sarah ran up to us. "Jenn, I heard you got into a fight with Judy Smith?"

"News sure travels fast around here, doesn't it?" Shayne asked me. I nodded.

"Yeah, I got into a little fight. Just shoving back and forth. That was basically it. Nothing major. It'll be old news by Monday," I said.

"I gotta get to class. I'm spending the night at your house tonight, okay?" she said, walking away.

"Doesn't she ever go anywhere besides our home?" Shayne asked.

"Nope," I said.

"Patrick likes her," Shayne said as the second bell rang. We started towards the math hall.

"He does? How do you know?" I asked.

"He told me. Plus they're always flirting. It's enough to make someone sick," he laughed.

I laughed too.

Shayne knocked on the door and asked for Patrick. "C'mon, little buddy. You gotta set up a jumping course so your sister can practice."

"I get outta school?" Patrick asked, turning around, his eyes lighting up.

"Yeah. C'mon," Shayne said.

Patrick stuffed his books into his bag and jumped up, not asking for his homework. He probably wouldn't do it anyway. He just didn't do homework on weekends. But he made such good grades on everything else, he didn't need to. Or at least that's what he told me.

We went to the front office, Shayne signed us out, and then we loaded the truck and drove off.

"I've been thinkin' about gettin' a new car," Shayne said.

"What kind?" Patrick asked.

"I dunno. I just need something besides this truck," Shayne shrugged.

I knew what he was thinking. His girlfriend was tired of being carted around in a dirty truck. I didn't blame her. She had an original name - Desiree. She was real pretty with short dark hair and dark hazel eyes. She was really nice to me and sometimes we went trail riding together – her, Sarah and I. She was nineteen. Shayne really liked her and I kept wondering when they were ever gonna finally get married. I knew that was on both their minds, but neither of them had the guts to say anything. But I didn't say any of this to Shayne because I wasn't sure of his reaction.

"Hey baby Sis, what'd ya do to your lip?" was Patrick's next question.

"I got into a little shove fight with Judy," I answered, stressing the word "little."

"Hey, ain't she Skyler Johnson's girl?"

"Yep."

Patrick snickered. "I know her. Can't stand her, but I know her. Whatever she got she deserved it."

"That's what I said," Shayne put in. "Said it right to their faces."

"Whose face?" Patrick asked, very interested.

"Her parents and Stephens. He's always hated me. He gave me O.S.S. a couple of years ago when I got into trouble for something; I don't even remember what it was now. Wasn't fighting. But all I know was it was not my fault, but no one believed me," Shayne said.

"Well, this was my fault," I admitted.

"Oh, who cares?" Shayne mumbled. "Dad and Mr. Stephens never got along either. I think they went to school together and didn't get along very well."

I realized then that he hadn't stuck up for me completely. He was still sore because the principal had done something to him before and he was just telling him what the thought of him. He was also sticking up for our Dad. I suddenly wished I had never shoved Judy.

Patrick reached across me and turned on the radio. That boy and his music...

Chapter 23

Patrick and Sarah

. When we got home, Patrick and I didn't get to watch TV or have free time. We were put to work, as usual. I got to mow the lawn and rake it, while Patrick got the pleasure of cleaning the stables, again. We had lunch at 1:00 and then we got to set up the hurdles. Shayne took one of the horses and went to check the cattle. We do that from time to time. Patrick and I were in the middle of setting up hurdles when Shayne came riding up. Patrick and I walked over to the fence.

"What's up?" Patrick asked.

"There's a cow out there gettin' ready to have a calf, but I can't get to her. She won't let me. I need your help, Pat. C'mon," Shayne said.

Patrick climbed the fence as I asked, "Can't she have it on her own?"

"I'm not sure. She hasn't had one before," Shayne answered. "Patrick! Hurry up!"

Patrick came riding bareback out of the stable. Shayne kicked his horse and they galloped off. I shrugged and went back to setting up hurdles. It took a long time, setting them up by myself, but eventually I got it done. I got bored, so I went to swing on the rope swing. I climbed up into the loft and swung for a while. It made my stomach jump because it felt like I was just falling and then all of a sudden I was caught and rising upwards. It was fun, like riding a rollercoaster or something. I got kind of lost, swinging in the barn, in my own little world. I got snapped out of it when Danny yelled, "Wee!" I almost fell off the swing.

"You scared me!" I yelled at him, only half-angry.

"Well, that's what you're here for isn't it?" Danny laughed, "For us to pick on?"

"Oh shut up." I waited for the swing to slow down, then jumped out of it.

"Hey, here comes Patrick and Shayne," Danny said, looking out the door.

They came riding into the barn and Patrick had something on the back of his horse. He dismounted, then got it down. It was the calf.

"Oh! It's so cute!" I exclaimed.

"Ain't it?" Patrick smiled.

"We had to shoot the mother," Shayne said, regretfully.

"Oh, no. You did?" I asked.

Shayne nodded.

"I'll go get one of the bottles so that we can feed it," Danny said and ran off.

I bent down, petting it. The poor thing. It was so tiny and frail. It just stood trembling. It looked so sad I almost felt like crying. But things like that happen on ranches, and I was used to it. "Poor thing," I whispered.

"It'll probably die too," Shayne mumbled.

"Not if we take care of it," I said.

"Suit yourself," he shrugged and rode out of the barn.

"I didn't know he had a gun with him," I said.

"He usually carries one when he goes to check the cattle. Didn't you see the case on his saddle?" Patrick asked.

"I guess not." I answered, still petting the calf.

"Here, Jenn. You want to feed it?" Danny asked, offering the bottle to me.

"Sure," I said.

I tried to get it to eat, but the calf refused. Patrick tried, too, but it didn't work.

"Let's put it in an empty stall with some extra straw. We can come back out here after supper," Patrick suggested.

"Okay," I said.

We put a lot of straw in a stall near the door and put the calf in there. It laid down, not able to stand any longer.

"Do you think it'll make it?" I asked softly.

"I dunno. C'mon. Let's go eat," Patrick said, "Sarah's here."

We left the calf in the stall with the extra hay, but I still felt guilty leaving it there.

"Jennifer!" Sarah ran over to me.

"Hey," I said. "Hungry?"

"Did you really have to ask?" Patrick asked from behind me.

"Shut up!" Sarah yelled at him.

"You're always hungry," Patrick said and ran into the house.

"Why don't you all just - nevermind," I sighed.

"Why don't we just what?" Sarah asked.

"Nothin'. I'll tell ya later," I said.

"Tell me!" she begged.

"Later," I said, going into the house.

"You're mean," she mumbled and punched my back.

"Ouch. Don't," I said.

"Ha!" she ran ahead of me into the kitchen.

"Brat," I mumbled to myself.

"I heard that!" she yelled back to me.

"I don't care!" I called after her. I walked into the kitchen and sat down.

"Where are your Grandparents?" Sarah asked.

"They went on a trip with a group from our church. I can't believe they left us here to take care of the ranch," Blake answered.

"You've still got me and the farm hands around," Olive said, setting water glasses on the table.

"Goody," Jeremy mumbled.

"Hush," Olive said.

We began to eat, pretty much in silence, until Sarah cried, "Ouch!"

Patrick grinned. Sarah kicked him under the table and they played "footsie" until Shayne yelled at both of them to knock it off. Sarah stuck out her bottom lip and pretended to pout.

"I can't wait until tomorrow. The jumping competition and show are gonna be so much fun!" Shawn exclaimed. He always got excited and hyper before a show.

"Yeah, and the rodeo on Sunday!" Patrick put in.

"I am gonna beat Skyler Johnson so bad, it won't even be funny. Well, at least not for him," I said.

"You just better hope you win," Sarah said, "Or you'll be shoveling double over time and be outta money."

"Out of money?" Shayne asked.

"Yeah she and Judy Smith made a bet that - oops!" Sarah clapped a hand over her own mouth.

"A what?" Shayne asked me.

I slouched down as far as I could in my chair. I tried to kick Sarah under the table, but all I did was bump my shin against the table leg. "It was just a little bet," I mumbled.

"How much?" Shayne asked.

"Just a little," I said again.

"How much?" Shayne repeated, his voice growing angry.

"A hundred bucks?" I half whispered.

"Call it off," he said sternly.

"What? But, Shayne-" I started.

"Call..it..off!" he paused between each word. "Right now. Call her and tell her it's off. I don't want you to have anything to do with that family. Call her, tell her the bet's off and hang up."

Reluctantly, I got up and went to the phone. I dialed her number and waited for her to pick up.

"Hello?"

I cringed and said," Judy, this is Jennifer."

"What do you want?" she asked in the most snobbish voice I had ever heard.

"My brother found out about the bet and I have to call it off."

"Well, fine. I don't really care."

"But only the money part. The part about cleaning stables still stands," I said. I did not really care if Shayne agreed with me on that.

"Like I said, I don't really care. I just hope you enjoy cleaning stables that much."

"It's you that's gonna be cleaning stalls," I argued.

"Well, whatever," she sighed. "I have someone more important on the other line, so I have to go."

"Good." I hung up.

Shayne shook his head and looked at the floor.

"What?" I asked.

He looked up laughing. "You are gonna get whooped. Skyler is one of the best jumpers around. Get out your shovel."

"Oh, shut up. Hey, where'd Danny go?" I asked, suddenly realizing he wasn't there.

"I think he went outside to take care of that calf," Bryson answered.

"Oh," I said as I sat down to finish my supper.

After dinner I went out to the barn. Danny was out there with the calf.

"Can't you get it to eat?" I asked quietly.

Danny shook his head slowly, sadly. "Nope," he whispered.

"Poor little thing," I said.

Danny was on his knees, petting the calf which lay trembling in the straw. "I think it's cold," he said. He pushed some straw up around it and went to get some more from the loft. He threw down a bale and hauled it over to the stall. He untied the wire and spread the straw in around the calf.

"C'mon, let's go inside," I suggested.

"You go ahead. I'm gonna stay out here a little longer," Danny said.

"All right, what's the matter with you?" I asked.

"Nothin', Jenn. Just leave me alone for a little while, okay?"

"Are you sure?"

"I'm positive. Just go." Danny sounded almost angry, so I went.

I turned in the doorway. "If you need anything or wanna talk to me, my door is always open."

"Thanks," he said.

I walked back to the house. It was already dark outside and it was getting colder. I shivered.

"It's getting cold," I said as I walked in the house.

"Help! Help me!" someone screamed from the living room.

I ran to see what was the matter. "What?"

"Help!"

Patrick and Blake had Sarah pinned on the floor and were tickling her.

"You all are idiots!" I declared and stormed out of the room. I decided I didn't want to go to bed alone so I called, "Sarah! Let's go to bed! I'm tired!"

"Comin'!" she yelled and ran up to me.

"Hey, wait!" Patrick hollered and came over to where we were standing. "Sarah, go on. I need to talk to Jenn."

"No! I am staying right here!" Sarah stomped her foot.

"I'm serious," he said.

"Oh. Okay. Nightie - night," she waved and ran up the stairs.

"Jennifer, I need to ask you a favor," Patrick started.

"Paddy, I'm really tired. Can this wait until the morning?" I griped.

"No, it'll only take a minute. Um... will you ask Sarah out for me?" he asked, sheepishly.

I sighed exhasperatedly. "It is about time. Yes, I'll ask her for you."

"I love you Baby Sis," he said and hugged me.

"I know. You owe me now, you know that, right?" I asked as I started up the stairs.

"Big time," he answered and ran back to the living room.

"The things I do for that boy," I mumbled to myself as I opened the door to my room.

"Do for who?" Sarah asked, looking at my trophies.

"Patrick," I said.

"What'd my cutiepatootie want?" she asked.

"Your cutiepa- nevermind," I shook my head. "He wants to know if you'll go out with him."

"What?" Sarah looked at me wide eyed.

"I asked, will you go out with Patrick?"

"Yes!" she exclaimed, bouncing up and down on her toes.

"Calm down, he didn't ask you to marry him," I said.

"Not yet," she giggled and threw herself onto my bed.

"Oh, my gosh," I mumbled. I opened the door and yelled at the top of my lungs, "Patrick, Sarah said yes!"

I hear a muffled, "Woo-hoo!" as I closed the door.

"You did not just-" Sarah started.

"Oh, but I did," I smiled as I clicked off the light.

"Brat!" A pillow was thrown and hit me in the face. I grabbed it and hit Sarah with it.

"No more!" she yelled.

"Off the bed," I said.

"I'm leaving!" Sarah yelled and left my room.

I changed into my pajamas and got into bed. I stared up at the glow stars on my ceiling, trying to fall asleep. I was so nervous about the next day; I tossed and turned all night. It took me at least two hours before I finally fell asleep.

Chapter 24

Getting Ready for Competition

The next morning, they let Shawn and I sleep in late so that we would be ready for the competition. Danny woke us up at 7:30 and I ate a late breakfast. I was still a little bit sleepy as Shawn and I ate, but he was practically bouncing off the walls.

"Calm down," I yawned.

"I can't!" he declared.

"Why? I am still tired," I said.

"Tired? You'd betta wake up, dawg!" he said, raising one hand in the air.

"Don't do that. You look stupid," I said.

"Well aren't we little miss positivity this morning?" he asked sarcastically. "I know someone who woke up on the wrong side of the bed this morning!"

"Leave me alone," I mumbled.

"No," he laughed and threw a piece of orange at me.

"Ah! You brat!" I threw it back at him, laughing. We were having fun throwing fruit at each other until Olive saw us and hollered for us to stop.

"Well, I'd better go get a shower," Shawn sighed and got up from the table.

"Not if I get there first!" I yelled and ran for the door.

"No way!" he called after me.

I didn't stand a chance. He had me half way up the stairs, then grabbing the collar of my shirt, pulled me back so fast that I fell down the stairs and he ran ahead and the next thing I heard was the loud bang of the bathroom door as he slammed it shut.

"Are you all right?" Olive asked, looking out of the kitchen to where I sat at the bottom of the stairs.

"Yeah. Where's everyone?" I asked.

"I don't know. I think Shayne's still asleep. Will you go into the basement and wake him up?" Olive asked.

"Yeah," I sighed. The door to the basement was right next to the stairs. I stood up and opened the door. "Shayne! Wake up!" I yelled down the stairs.

"Jennifer! Go down there and wake him up. Don't yell down there the way Danny does," Olive scolded me.

"Oh, okay," I mumbled. I walked down the stairs. It was dim in the basement because the only light came from two small windows just above Shayne's bed. His weights were near the end of the bed, which sat to the right of the creaky old wooden stairs leading to the cold cement floor. He had a large dresser on the wall between the bed and the stairs. He kept all his old clothes in it, and put his good clothes in the small closet near the dresser. To the left he had an old couch and a recliner facing a television. He had a refrigerator on the far end and a table with chairs and even an oven. I liked it in Shayne's room. Shayne lay on his stomach, the blankets thrown this way and that, his feet hanging out from under them and over the edge of the bed. He always slept in shorts and thick socks pulled up to his knees. "Shayne," I said in a quiet voice, shaking his shoulder.

"Go away," came a muffled answer from the pillow.

"Wake up," I said.

"Go away!" It was a little clearer this time.

I knew how to get him up. "But the cows are out!"

"What?" he rolled over and sat up.

"Ha, ha!" I laughed, "Got ya."

"You're mean," he yawned. "I guess I gotta get up, huh?"

"Brilliant deduction, Sherlock," I said.

"Why, thank you Wattson," he said as he got up. He walked to the closet and looked through it. He always dressed up for competitions or other occasions.

I picked up one of the twenty-pound weights and put it on the bench press. I could press almost eighty pounds because I was used to lifting feed bags and hay bales. I laid down and started to lift the weights. "Look Shayne," I said, "I'm buff."

He turned to look at me and laughed. "Wanna fight?" he asked, flexing his arm and showing off his muscles.

"Oh, heck, no," I said.

"Why aren't you getting ready for your competition?" he asked.

"Because Shawn got to the bathroom first," I fake-sobbed.

"Did he now?" Shayne asked, pulling on a shirt with a laugh.

"Yes. We need another bathroom," I suggested.

"Maybe that'll be my next project," he said.

"It needs to be," I said. It was getting harder for me to lift the weights.

"I ain't doin' it alone," he said, pulling on black boots.

"Help," I said. I couldn't lift the weights anymore and I was afraid I was going to drop them on myself and crack my ribs. That was the last thing I needed for the day.

"You'll help me?" he asked.

"No! Help me!"

"Huh? Oh!" Shayne ran to help me when he saw how I was struggling with the weights. He lifted them with one arm and put them where they belonged. "You all right?"

"Whoo. Yeah," I sighed with a little giggle.

"Olive!" I heard Shawn's muffled voice from up stairs. "Where are my clothes for the competition?"

"Sounds like he's outta the shower. Go get your shower now and I'm gonna go out and clean the tack up for you both one more time before the show," Shayne said.

"Okay," I said and left the basement. I made a run for the bathroom before anyone else could get there and slammed the door shut behind me.

I got dressed and had my hair fixed. Sarah did my hair for me. She made it into a bun at the back of my neck. I wore khaki colored riding pants, a hunter green riding jacket, black gloves, and shiny black boots. I walked out of the house and down to the stables, keeping my back as straight and proper as possible. When I got there, Shawn had the reins of Eclipse and Patrick was waiting for me with Thundering Glory. Patrick looked like a plain country bumpkin next to Shawn. Shawn was wearing white riding pants, new black boots and a bright red riding jacket.

"Hey, hey, hey!" Jeremy declared, coming into the stables. He was holding the video camera.

"Oh no, it's you," Shawn mumbled.

"Hey, how 'bout a little respect here for your official cameraman?" Jeremy asked.

"His future job," I muttered to myself.

Jeremy always video-recorded all of our events because, as I mentioned earlier, he didn't rodeo or do any other events on horseback. He had a regular camera on a strap around his neck.

"Okay," he said, "Let's get a picture of the two winners and their horses!"

I took Thundering Glory's reins and stood beside Shawn. Patrick went to stand behind Jeremy.

He whistled over and over quickly to get the horses to look towards the camera.

"Say cheese!" Jeremy laughed.

Shawn and I smiled. The bright flash near blinded me and I saw spots in front of my eyes for a while.

"Here are your helmets and crops," Danny ran into the barn.

"Crop?" I asked. "I don't wanna use that on Thundering Glory."

"So don't. Just hold it. It looks better," Danny said with a smile.

"Okay," I said. I took the crop from Danny and my helmet. I put the helmet on and fastened it under my chin. I held the crop in my left hand. A crop is a short whip used in jumping competitions and sometimes in shows.

Shawn put his helmet on and took his crop from Danny.

"Dude, there are a bunch of people here," Jeremy said, looking out of the door through the video camera.

"Well, let's go," Shawn said. He led Eclipse out first and I followed.

"Jeremy, you'd better get that camera out of my face!" I said and slapped his leg with the crop.

"Don't!" He stopped to rub his leg.

"Jennifer!" a voice called from behind me.

I turned around. "Christian!"

Christian grinned at me from Tex's back.

"What are you doing here?" I asked. I had forgotten that he and his family had planned to stay at the ranch until it closed.

"Well, I heard you were having a major competition today and I thought I'd stop by and see how you and that horse of yours would do," He said, dismounting.

"That's so sweet," I smiled.

Christian walked over to me. "This is for good luck." He kissed me quickly on the cheek.

It surprised me so much that all I could stutter was, "Th-thank you."

Christian turned red in the face and looked at the ground.

"Aw! How sweet!" Jeremy called.

"You did not!" I cried.

"I did," he laughed, holding the video camera in the air.

"Patrick! Murder him for me!" I yelled.

Patrick came up from behind Jeremy and, grabbing him by the shoulders, pulled him away into the mix of riders, horses, trucks and trailers.

"I'm sorry about him," I mumbled.

"That's okay," Christian said. We stood in silence for a little while then he said, "Hey, guess what. My Mom's thinkin' about movin' here."

"Really? Where do you live right now?" I asked.

"Arkansas. I think I'd like it better here, though. I'd probably even go to the same school as you and, I think her name's Alissa?"

"Oh, Alissa lives in North Carolina. But Sarah goes to school with me."

"Sarah, hmm, don't know her."

"Oh, well, anyway, you'll get to know her if you move within fifty miles from here. Everyone knows Sarah," I laughed.

"Hey, there's Skyler," Christian said, nodding behind me.

"Oh, mm-hmm."

"What? You don't like him anymore?"

"Not since his girlfriend and I met."

"You don't like her?"

"We don't get along too well."

"You're jealous, aren't you?"

"What? No!" The question took me by surprise.

"Oh. Well, I-"

"Hello, Jennifer," came a snobby voice from behind me.

"Go away, Judy," I said through clenched teeth without even turning around.

"Well, fine. I was just coming to say good luck," she said.

"You're the one that needs luck," I muttered.

"Dream on. Oh, who's this? Your boyfriend?" she asked.

"Judy, please go away," I said.

"Okay, fine," she held her hands in the air innocently. "I'll go." She turned and walked away.

"Is that her?" Christian asked.

"Yes," I mumbled.

"Snob," he said.

I laughed. "You wanna ride around for a little while before the competition starts? It's almost another hour before it even starts. I wanna go look at the sales barns and see what kinds of horses they have over there."

"Sure," he said.

I mounted Thundering Glory and Christian remounted Tex and we rode over to the barns.

Chapter 25

The Competition

An hour later, we rode back to the arena. There were several more people there. I saw so many beautiful horses; I could not believe it.

"There you are!" Shayne exclaimed. He was very dressed up in dress pants and a nice shirt. His hair was neatly combed.

"I went over to the sales barns," I explained.

"Did you see anything that you like?" he asked.

"Not really," I answered.

"Well, I hope you're ready. I think the first competition's about to start. Here, I got your number," Patrick said, walking towards us, holding up my riding number. "Get off and let me pin it to the back of your shirt."

I dismounted and let Patrick pin it to my jacket. "What number is it?"

"102," he answered. "Hold still!"

"All right, all right," I murmured.

"There ya go," he said, proud of himself.

“It better not be crooked,” I warned.

The voice over the loudspeaker came on. "Welcome, everyone! We are pleased that you have all come out here today..."

"You'd better mount up. Warm the horse up," Shayne suggested.

"C'mon, Sis, let's ride around and show off a bit, eh?" Shawn walked up on Eclipse next to me.

"Okay," I said. I mounted and Shawn and I started to walk our horses. My stomach was doing flip-flops and I got so dizzy with nervousness I thought for a minute that I was going to fall off my horse.

"Whoa, you okay?" Shawn asked, grabbing hold of my arm, as if to keep me from falling.

"Yeah, I'm just nervous is all. I'll be okay."

"Don't be nervous. Just chill, man," he said in a smooth voice.

"Oh, shut up," I laughed.

He stuck his tongue out at me.

"We are now preparing for our first division; riders ages eighteen and up. Will these riders please come to the arena and be ready to perform when they are called upon?" The voice blared over the loudspeaker.

"That's me. Wish me luck," Shawn said as he turned Eclipse towards the arena.

"Good luck!" I called after him as he cantered away. I decided to watch him and trotted over to near the arena.

A girl on a dapple was jumping. She was doing really good, jumping pretty fast, but she knocked a post off on one of her last jumps. Still, she got a good time.

"Next up is number 117, Shawn Blackwell, on his seven year old gray mare, Eclipse," the announcer said.

Shawn cantered into the arena. He had a pretty good run through. He went all clear (meaning he did not knock any of the poles off of the jumps) but there was one rider that went fast and clear. There were nine riders in all, Shawn placed second. He trotted out of the arena, a red ribbon hanging from the left side of Eclipse's bridle. "Ah, we'll get her next time, won't we girl?" he asked, stroking the horse's neck. Eclipse nickered as if to say, "Of course we will."

"Now riders ages fourteen through seventeen will compete. There are seven riders in this division..." the loudspeaker announced.

"That's me," I said and took a few shallow breaths as I mounted.

"It'll be okay," Shawn said. "Just like in practice."

"Yeah, Jenn. You'll do fine," Shayne said.

"Besides, you deserve to win more than anyone else."

"Bryson? What are you doing here?" I asked in shock.

"I decided to come and watch you perform. You've worked hard. Good luck," Bryson said.

"Thanks," I smiled. It meant a lot to me to have Bryson come and watch. Like I have said before, Bryson hated horses. He usually just stayed home when we went to any sort of competition or rodeo.

I trotted over near the gate. I was getting really nervous and I think Thundering Glory could tell. My hands were shaky and clammy and my legs were trembling. I tried to make my legs stop, but the effort was pointless. Until I saw Judy. She was standing next to Skyler and he was holding the reins to his horse. She was hanging all over him.

"You ain't gotta prayer," a voice said beside me.

"Go away," I said.

"You don't stand a chance against my brother," Jonah went on, ignoring me.

"I have a good horse and I've worked hard. I can do whatever I put my mind to," I said, trying to avoid conflict.

"You still don't stand a chance," he repeated.

"Will you just go away?"

"No."

"I figured," I mumbled.

"What?"

"Nothin'," I said.

"Well, fine. I'm a-goin' then," he said and walked away.

"My brother is always rude like that," Skyler said.

"I didn't even see you ride up," I said, turning to look at him. He was sitting on a white horse beside me. There was already a rider in the arena, jumping.

"Obviously. You were to busy arguing with my brother," he said.

"Won't Judy get upset if she sees you talking to me?" I asked.

"Huh? Oh. She's over at the truck, talking on the car phone," he said.

"Oh, so you can only talk to me when she isn't within ear or eye shot."

"You don't talk to me."

"Because I don't want to be around her."

"Why?"

"Why what?"

"Why don't you want to be around her?"

"Why would I? She treats everyone like dirt, Skyler, and you know it. She's a two-faced, snotty, little brat. I don't want to have anything to do with her."

"I guess she is a little rude at times-"

"A little?" I scoffed.

"Okay, a lot of the time," he said with a slight chuckle in his voice. "But she's good down deep."

"Yeah right," I murmured.

"She's a lot like you," he said.

"Oh, please! How in the world could you possibly think that?"

"I bet you aren't as tough as you come across as. You're soft down deep. Otherwise you wouldn't have kept that horse," he said.

I bit my lower lip. "You're right," I admitted quietly.

"See?" he smiled.

"But that still doesn't mean I have to have anything to do with your snobby girlfriend!" I declared.

Skyler started to say something, but the loudspeaker interfered. "Next up is number 102, Jennifer Blackwell, on her three year old stallion, Thundering Glory."

"Gotta go," I said and went through the gate.

"Good luck!" someone yelled. I think it was Skyler...

I did well. Thundering Glory went fast and clear. After my turn was over, I felt better. I never used the crop once.

"Good job," Shawn congratulated me as I dismounted.

"Thanks," I said. I was breathing hard. The next rider was halfway through the routine. "I got really nervous the first couple of jumps," I panted, "but then I was okay."

"Are you all right?" Patrick asked.

"I'm okay. I'm just a little nervous still," I said. "I'm not used to this. I like just lettin' the horse go and try to stay on."

"That's what I'm sayin'," Patrick laughed.

"Next up is number 206, Skyler Johnson, on his four year old mare, White Liberty," the loudspeaker announced.

"I'm gonna go watch Skyler. Take him," I handed the reins to Patrick and ran over to the arena. Skyler was going over the second jump, going unusually slow. I watched his hands carefully as he cantered. I was astonished. I cannot even describe what I thought as I watched him perform. If White Liberty would try to speed up, Skyler would tell her to slow down with a slow movement of the reins. Skyler was cheating for me! He hid it well, but watching as carefully as I was, I could tell. He finished, going clear and got a fairly good time, but it was still slower than mine was. He and I both knew it. He came out of the arena smiling. I stood watching in shock.

"How'd I do?" he asked, smiling down at me from White Liberty's back.

"You-" I started.

"Skyler! That was wonderful!" Judy ran up to him. "I'm positive you beat that scroungy black thing she was riding." Judy looked directly at me as she said this.

"Don't get your hopes too high. I did the best I could," Skyler said as he dismounted. I knew he was lying.

"Well, if you lose to any of these other riders, the judge is absolutely blind," she said and gave a short giggle. It was so fakc I almost got sick.

"Hey, isn't that Mandy over there?" Skyler asked, nodding towards Jeremy. Mandy was hanging on Jeremy's arm while he was trying to video-record Patrick doing a handstand.

"Oh, I'm gonna go say hi," Judy said and walked away.

Skyler turned back to me. "So, what's up?"

"Did you- I mean- oh! Nevermind," I didn't know what to say.

"Yeah, I was cheating for you," he answered my question without my even asking it.

"But, why?" I asked.

"To make shut Judy up. I like her and everything, but I like you too and I'm sick of her being so mean to you," he said.

"Like me?" I asked.

"As a friend."

"But you never even talk to me!" I exclaimed.

Skyler shrugged. "I've gotta go," he said and mounted White Liberty again.

"Okay. See ya," I said as he trotted away.

"What was that about?" Christian asked, walking up.

"I'm not exactly sure," I answered.

"Well, you'd better get your horse. That's the last rider in there. They'll be announcing the winner, announcing you, I mean, in a few minutes."

"You've lost it," I laughed as we walked over to Patrick and Shayne. "Gimme my horse!"

"Meow! Hiss! Hiss!" Patrick exclaimed as he handed me the reins.

"You have no idea," I said and mounted.

"Hissssss!" he said again.

"Shayne, sick a dog on him or somethin'," I said and turned Thundering Glory towards the arena.

The loudspeaker announced for us to re-enter the arena. We lined up and I ended up between Skyler and a girl who was riding a dark bay mare. The microphone gave a high pitched squeal, then popped a couple of times before the announcer could go on.

"Third place in this competition goes to Emily Brown on her horse, Firefly." One of the judges placed a yellow ribbon on the horse's bridle as the crowd applauded. "Second place goes to Skyler Johnson on his horse, White Liberty." The same judge placed a red ribbon on Skyler's horse. "And first place goes to Jennifer Blackwell on her horse, Thundering Glory." The judge placed a blue ribbon on Thundering Glory's bridle. I could feel myself beaming. I wished I could have seen Judy's face as they announced it. Skyler and I trotted out of the arena. Patrick and Blake were hanging over the red gate, whooping and hollering as if I had just made the whistle while bull riding.

"You two are both nuts!" I yelled at them as I trotted by.

"It seems to run in the family!" Blake called after me.

I trotted to an area that was less crowded before I dismounted. "Good boy," I whispered as I stroked Thundering Glory's neck.

Blake and Patrick ran up to me. "Woo-hoo! You rock, Baby Sis!" Patrick exclaimed.

"You da man! I mean, woman!" Blake corrected himself and laughed.

"Good job," Skyler said, riding up beside us.

"Skyler!" Judy shouted marching over to where we were standing.

"What?" he asked.

"You lost to her! How could you lose to her?" Judy demanded, almost in tears.

"I don't know," Skyler shrugged.

"You don't know anything, do you?" she asked angrily.

"Hey Judy," Patrick said.

"Huh?" she asked and looked at him.

He made movement with his arms, acting like he was shoveling out stalls.

Her eyes narrowed and she looked so mean it was almost scary.

"I could have done better," she said.

"You really think so?" I asked.

"I know so," she answered.

"Well, it wasn't the jumping, it was the speed. He was just a few seconds under my time," I said.

"So - what? Are you saying that you won just because your horse is faster than his?" she asked.

"Something like that," I answered.

"That is so stupid!" she exclaimed.

"Well, why don't you all race this afternoon to see who should have really won?" Skyler suggested.

"Man, you're just sore that you lost," Patrick said as Sarah walked up beside him. "She doesn't hafta race you and she ain't gonna race with -"

"Patrick! I can speak for myself," I stopped him. "I think it's a wonderful idea. I'll race you any day."

"But Judy thinks she can do better. You can race against her," Skyler said then smiled, very proud of himself.

"Even better," I said.

"Chick, you're askin' for trouble," Bryson said, walking up.

"He...he...he," I fake laughed. "Shut up."

"As soon as these competitions are over we're gonna race and I'm gonna show you that this horse is better than that one, no questions asked," Judy said, her nose up in the air.

"We'll see about that," I said.

"Where are you racin' at?" Sarah asked.

"Hey, we can go out in that old pasture, the one with the creek and the woods and stuff? That's an awesome place to race. Danny and I race out there a lot," Blake suggested.

"All right, the old pasture it is. Right after the competitions are over," Skyler said. He gave a quick, short smile at me. Judy mounted behind Skyler and they trotted away.

"Sarah, c'mere," I said in a quiet voice.

"What?" she asked as she walked over.

"Don't say anything to anyone. Skyler cheated for me. He let me win. I'm not sure if Thundering Glory can beat White Liberty," I whispered.

"Oh no. What are you going to do?" she asked.

"I have no clue..."

Chapter 26

Thundering Glory's Last Chance

"Okay. You go down to the post at the far end of the field. Then you go to the right and into the woods on the path. It's pretty wide, so it shouldn't be hard for you to both get through. You hafta jump the creek and then there's a long stretch that's downhill. It's pretty dangerous there, so be careful. You might wanna slow down. There's a bunch of rocks and things that are easy to trip over. Be careful. Then you go down through the clearing back into the woods, up another hill and then back here. The first one to make it back wins! Any questions?"

"Yeah, we gonna race or you gonna talk the rest of the day?" I asked. Even Judy laughed, sitting near me on White Liberty. She had on a riding helmet and held a crop in her hand. I knew she would use it, but there was nothing I could do about it.

"Hush up. We got people at certain points to make sure neither of you are cheating. If you get caught tryin' to cheat, ya lose," Shayne said.

"Shut up an' let 'em race!" Skyler declared. Skyler and Shayne were staying at the finish line to decide who would win. A couple of my brothers were at the points in the race as were Skyler's brothers.

"Okay! On your marks... get set... GO!" Shayne yelled as he pulled the trigger to the pistol.

I kicked Thundering Glory and we took off. Judy and I were neck and neck when we reached the post, but turning around, I got in the lead. It was not much of a lead, but at least I was ahead. The path through the woods was not near as wide as I had expected, but it was wide enough to ride on. We were both going so fast, yet the race seemed to take forever. I saw the creek and we jumped it easily. I was still a little ahead of Judy. I remembered the down hill part of our race. "Remember to slow down!" I warned Judy.

"Oh, you'd just love that, wouldn't you?" she yelled, almost even with me.

"Just slow down!" I reminded her.

"No way!"

We reached the hill and it was steeper than I thought it was going to be. I pulled back on Thundering Glory's reins. I was getting angry with Shayne for making the race seem easier than it actually was. There were trees on both sides of the path and even some in the middle of it. I slowed down even more, but Judy raced ahead. I moved more to the left to avoid hitting some trees. When I looked back to Judy's side, I was terrified. I had looked back just in time to see White Liberty trip over a large rock in the path. The horse fell on Judy's right leg and they both tumbled the rest of the way down the hill. I continued down the hill and stopped when I reached to bottom. She landed right at the beginning of the clearing. White Liberty was standing not too far away. She didn't look too hurt but she was limping slightly. I dismounted and ran to Judy's aid. She lay lifeless on the grass and for a moment I thought she was dead. But then, much to my relief, I realized she was breathing. "Judy? Judy, wake up!" I shook her shoulders, but she still laid unmoving on the damp grass.

"Jennifer! What happened?" Bryson ran over to me.

"Her horse tripped! She's hurt really bad," I exclaimed, my hands beginning to shake and my eyes stung like they were going to cry.

"Stay here. I'm gonna go get help." Bryson jumped up and took White Liberty's reins.

"You can't ride her! She's lame now!" I yelled at him.

Bryson looked at me, took a deep breath and said, "Okay." He grabbed Thundering Glory's reins and mounted quickly. "You stay here with her. I'll be back A.S.A.P!" he ordered and kicked Thundering Glory's sides and took off up the hill and was gone.

I did not know what to do, being left with Judy. I was really scared. I reached over and took her helmet off. Her right pant leg was shredded, as was her actual leg. It was bleeding badly. I took off my jacket and tied it around the worst part that was cut. I stayed right beside her the whole time. It was probably only about twenty-five minutes until anyone came, but it seemed like forever. There was not a breeze anywhere. The whole clearing was silent. Too silent for my liking. It was dead silent. I tried singing or something, but I was too upset for anything to come out of my mouth. Just when I thought I would go crazy from the silence, Bryson and Danny came down the hill on Thundering Glory and Double J, their hooves making a tremendous pounding that sounded like drums. Danny didn’t even wait for Double J to stop before he dismounted. I was thankful someone was finally there.

"Is she all right?" Danny asked.

"I don't know. I don't know," I answered quickly.

"The ambulance will be here in a minute," Bryson said. "I'm gonna go up the hill again and wait for them." He turned and started up the hill again.

"Thundering Glory will be exhausted before the day's over," I said.

"Jenn, do you even realize what Bryson's doing?" Danny asked, kneeling on the other side of Judy's body.

"What?"

"He's riding!" Danny exclaimed. "And he's even riding Thundering Glory!"

"He is, isn't he?" I smiled. "Did he hit his head too?"

"That's not funny," Danny replied.

"I know," I said.

Just then, a medical team came down the hill with a stretcher. They ordered us to get out of the way. Danny stood up and helped me up and we took a few steps back. They looked Judy over, using long medical terms that I didn't recognize. Then they placed her on the stretcher and, as quickly as possible, carried her up the hill.

Danny and I mounted Double J and followed closely behind. I held the reins to White Liberty's bridle and she obediently followed us.

The team put Judy into the ambulance and drove away. Danny and I sat and watched as they drove away. I slid backward off Double J and landed beside Skyler.

"It's my fault," he said miserably.

"It's not your fault. It was an accident. It could have happened to anyone," I said.

Skyler just looked away.

"Here's your horse," I held the reins out to him.

"Is she hurt?" he asked, taking them.

"Not too bad, I think," I answered.

Skyler looked her over. "Her leg's cut, but she'll be okay."

"I'm glad," I said.

"Listen, I'm sorry for all the trouble I've caused. If there's anyway I can make it up to you, let me know," Skyler said.

"It wasn't your fault," I said again. "You just go to the hospital and be with her. Call me and let me know how she is, all right?"

"Yeah. Sure. Thanks," he said and gave me a hug.

"You need a ride?" Shayne asked.

"Um, yeah," Skyler answered.

"C'mon. Get in the truck," Shayne motioned for Skyler to follow him. They walked away.

"Do you think she'll be okay?" Danny asked.

"I'm not sure. I hope so," I said. I kept remembering it over and over in my mind, seeing it as if it were a video rewinding then playing again, for my eyes only. I took a deep breath and shuddered.

"Let's go inside, Baby Sis," Blake said, walking up and putting his arm around my shoulder as Shayne and Skyler drove by.

"Do you think her parent's will sue us?" I asked.

"Don't worry about it," Blake said.

"Hey! What happened?" Christian asked, running up to us.

"C'mon inside and I'll tell you," I said as we walked towards the house.

"You okay?" he asked.

"Yeah," I answered. "Worse things have happened."

Chapter 27

One Year Later . . .

It has been almost a year since Judy was hurt. She hit her head and broke her leg and was in the hospital for a long time. Her parents decided not to sue, much to my Grandparents' relief. Judy is back in school and is back to her old, snobby self. She didn't learn anything, except not to mess with me anymore. . She was in the hospital for several months. She never tried to start anything with me again.

Shayne moved out of the house and got his own place and married Desiree, but he couldn't stay away from the ranch for long. They fixed up the basement and it is practically another whole house under there. It's really nice.

Sarah and Patrick are still dating, no surprise there. We will just have to wait and see what happens.

Christian and his mother did move here and he goes to my school now. He and Danny are really good friends.

Blake still continues to be creative and get into trouble. There is no hope for that boy.

Shawn moved out and is in the process of getting a business of his own going. He breeds, trains and shows horses for English shows and jumping competitions. He gets paid a lot of money for it too. He wanted me to move Thundering Glory out there, so that's where I spend a lot of my free time now. We have been working with Thundering Glory and Shawn is going to take him to nationals.

Jeremy has gone to college on a football scholarship.

I love riding English now. I jump all the time and I have even been in a couple of shows. I even bought a Tennessee Walker. But that does not mean I do not rodeo anymore. In fact, I bruised my ribs a few weeks ago on a bronco.

Oh, and I can't forget the biggest surprise. Bryson. He loves riding now. He even likes to rodeo. Did I say "likes"? I mean he loves to rodeo. He's almost worse than Patrick and I. I said almost...

About The Author

LINDSEY NICOLE TREGNAGO is a young author who enjoys art, reading, and horseback riding. She wrote her first book, Thundering Glory, when she was fourteen. Now, at the age of seventeen, she continues to write books while working as a Circulation Clerk at Little Dixie Regional Library.